THE PRINCESS OF THE ATOM

THE PRINCESS OF THE ATOM

RAY CUMMINGS

WILDSIDE PRESS

To my son, Hal,
and to Russ, my son-in-law
—both chemists—
this story is appropriately
and affectionately dedicated.

Originally published in 1929.
Published by Wildside Press, LLC.
Visit us online at wildsidepress.com.

INTRODUCTION

KARL WURF

Ray Cummings (1887–1957) was one of the pioneering voices of early American science fiction, sometimes described as the "father of scientific romance in the pulp era." Before turning to fiction, he worked as an assistant to Thomas Edison, an experience that left a deep impression on him. Edison's laboratory and the scientific advances of the late nineteenth and early twentieth centuries shaped Cummings's imagination, convincing him that fiction could bridge the gap between scientific theory and adventure storytelling. His writing often reflects the wonder of an age fascinated by electricity, chemistry, and atomic theory, combined with the dramatic flair of pulp magazines.

Cummings's early work appeared in *Argosy* and *All-Story Weekly*, at a time when magazines were shaping the foundation of modern science fiction. His breakthrough serial, *The Girl in the Golden Atom* (1919), exemplified his recurring theme: vast universes existing within the infinitesimal spaces of the atom. This imaginative exploration of scale—shrinking humans into atomic realms or enlarging them to giant proportions—was one of his lasting contributions to the genre. He shared with contemporaries like A. Merritt and Edgar Rice Burroughs a sense of wonder and a willingness to merge speculative science with romance and adventure.

While Cummings is best remembered for his atomic fantasies, his career also extended into the world of comic books. In the 1940s, he wrote for Timely Comics, the company that would later become Marvel. There he scripted adventures for *Captain America Comics* and other titles during the Golden Age of superheroes. His experience in pulp storytelling translated easily to comics, where the need for swift pacing, bold ideas, and cliffhanger drama was essential. Cummings was one of the writers who helped bridge the pulp magazine tradition with the emerging comic book industry.

In addition to science fiction and comics, Cummings wrote mysteries and romances, always keeping his prose brisk and accessible. His career spanned decades when the lines between popular fiction categories were fluid, and his versatility kept him in steady demand. Yet his reputation rests most strongly on his speculative visions of infinite smallness and vast largeness, ideas that anticipated later explorations of quantum worlds and alternate dimensions in both literature and film.

Readers interested in exploring more of his science fiction beyond *The Princess of the Atom* may turn to *The Girl in the Golden Atom*, which began his atomic saga; *Beyond the Vanishing Point*, another tale of shrinking into miniature worlds; *Brigands of the Moon*, an interplanetary adventure serialized in *Astounding Stories*; and *The Fire People*, which depicts strange invaders from the Sun. These works showcase the full range of Cummings's imagination, from microcosmic universes to cosmic voyages.

Cummings's place in literary history is secure as a key transitional figure: a writer who drew from the scientific optimism of Edison's age, carried it through the pulp era, and helped seed the comic book explosion. His stories remain both a record of early science fiction's themes and a testament to the enduring human urge to imagine worlds beyond our own.

PROLOGUE

I was seventeen years old before I had any idea that there was a mystery in my family. My name is Frank Ferrule. My mother died when I was still a child. There was my father; my older brother, Drake; and my younger sister, Dianne. We had always seemed to me an average little family group, except for Dianne's beauty. That, in truth, was abnormal enough. And upon that, I was to learn, the mystery hinged—tragedy it was for Dianne, striking all unheralded like a bolt from a cloudless sky.

Our life, up to that August when the sudden, inexplicable tragedy came, was perfectly prosaic, uneventful, so that I can find little of it to record here that would be of interest. Father was a consulting chemist. My brother Drake, six years older than I, grew up to be a stalwart blond giant of a fellow—a full six feet two—with a lazy, rollicking good-nature like a huge dog conscious of his own strength. Father often said that; and called me a terrier. I was always small and slender, with dark hair, and by nature excitable.

There was nothing unusual, nothing of particular interest about Drake and me. But Dianne's beauty would have fascinated the world. I can remember that she had always been beautiful. In the advertisements of fashion magazines there are drawings of children—ideally beautiful little girls. Dianne, as a child, was like that, a blue-eyed flaxen-haired doll.

But soon she began to develop character. At sixteen the doll look was wholly gone. Her face bore the stamp of her individuality; but it remained as exquisite, as colorful as a cameo, or like a pastel, so delicately flawless of feature, so perfect of natural coloring that the effect was startling. I have heard people say, meeting her, that she seemed unreal. And certainly, everywhere she went, she attracted unusual attention.

This tragedy came—the mystery began—one August when Dianne was sixteen, I seventeen, and Drake twenty-three. We were at our summer home on the coast of Maine. Father was of a temperament which demanded a quiet life. I think, too, that with such a girl as Dianne, he found seclusion an added advantage.

She could so easily have been spoiled; but she was not. A gentle little thing, sweet in the old-fashioned storied style, with all the sophistication of her age passing her by untouched. Mischievous she had always been since childhood, and she was human enough to be thrilled by the frequent offers of motion-picture tryouts and the like.

Such offers inevitably came. We were not hermits. We spent our winters in New York City. Quietly, but we had many friends and the fame of Dianne's beauty spread.

But father kept her unspoiled, and apart from it all.

We often had friends at our summer home; but it chanced that this particular August there was no one but our family there. I recall the fateful morning of the fourteenth. There was nothing to mark it from any other morning—warm and cloudless, with a fresh breeze that rippled the water of the cove and set the whitecaps running outside.

Father announced that he would be all day at a chemical experiment and not to disturb him. Drake, Dianne and I decided that we would take the dory and row out to Bird's Nest Island; fish a little; have a swim and a campfire lunch. We started soon after breakfast. It was not a long pull, for the island was only some two miles offshore. We found the sea outside smooth running, but brisk. The wide bow of the dory lifted and slapped as we headed into the whitecaps.

Bird's Nest Island had, to my mind, always spelled romance. It was a tiny, rocky peak alone in the sea, an irregularly round island only a few hundred acres in extent. The fifty-foot peak was almost in its center. Gulls often hung around that little naked crag pointing skyward. A rocky, but gently sloping beach encircled all the island. There were trees and underbrush; and, strangely enough, a spring of fresh water.

It was an uninhabited island, with all the romance of Robinson Crusoe hanging over it. From the rock peak one could stand and see all the circular island shore and the sea in every direction. As children we had come here with the grownups. We had placed a cairn upon the summit and erected a signal flag, then, ignoring the obvious shore of the Maine coast, had built a signal fire and prayed that its smoke might be seen by some passing ship which would come and rescue us.

We were too old for such fancies now, but the romance clung. We put on our swimming suits, this August morning, and swam from the lee beach. There is only one incident of significance for me to record.

Drake was swimming far out with lusty strokes. Dianne and I not so skillful or daring in the water, were in the shallows of the beach. I recall that I leaped at her and ducked her. She came up gasping, but laughing, and made a rush at me. We mingled in a fight, tumbling each other into the water.

I had always been Dianne's favorite. We were nearer an age, and Drake, when in his 'teens, had looked down upon us as mere children. We wrestled now in the water; and I remember that I found myself clinging to Dianne's hair, up by her forehead.

"Frank, stop that! Let me go!"

The frightened vehemence of her tone made me loose her at once.

"What's the matter?"

"You hurt me."

"Shucks."

A girl growing up with two older brothers gets used to rough treatment. It was not like Dianne to call quits.

"You did hurt me."

"Did I? Sorry, Dianne. Come on, let's swim then. Look where Drake is."

The incident left me puzzled. Dianne had done that before. She did not like her hair touched. It grew down at the center of her forehead in a little peak, and she wore it parted far to one side.

Children are not curious about such things, but I was old enough now to wonder why Dianne was annoyed when her hair there was touched.

Drake came ashore, and he and I wandered off to dress. Then we called to Dianne. We had left her only a couple of hundred feet away.

I called, "Oh Dianne, hurry it up. You going to take all day?"

She did not answer. We called again. Drake said, "She's spoofing us. Hiding."

We ran back to where we had left her. The little pile of her clothes lay there untouched.

"Dianne!" Our shouts echoed over the island, but there was no answer.

"Find her in two minutes," said Drake. He shouted, "Watch out, Dianne, we're coming! I'll run around the beach first, Frank. You climb up to the rock—see everything from there—"

I went up to the peak, where I could see all the beach. Our dory was undisturbed, and I could see no sign of a boat leaving the island, or anywhere near it. I saw Drake sprinting around the beach, then plunging off among the trees. I could see his figure occasionally. He called up:

"See her, Frank?"

"No!"

Fear struck us then. We searched, at first laughingly, then with stark horror overwhelming us. The little island was all too easy to search. There were no caves, no cliff over which she could have fallen. We had seen all the beach and the near-by water within a few moments after her disappearance. Surely there had not been time for her to swim out and be drowned. She was a fair swimmer, and cautious for all her youth. And even if she had gone back in the water and got into distress, we were so close we could have heard at once any call she made.

But she was gone. Vanished. No boat had landed that could have taken her. That was impossible without our seeing it over that reach of empty sea.

I recall our frantic search. Then at last Drake and I alone frantically rowed back home to tell father. It was like a dream of horror. Father's white, solemn face. He never once reproached Drake or me. He telephoned the village. Then came another trip to the island in a launch with grave-faced men.

But Dianne was never found. We brought back her clothes that lay untouched there by the underbrush at the beach. I could not look at them, but went into my bedroom and lay on the bed and sobbed. It was the first tragedy that life had brought me.

Night had fallen when Drake came to me. He leaned over me sympathetically.

"Take it easy, kid." His own face was white and drawn; he loved Dianne as much as I did, but he was older, more stoical. "Father wants to see us, Frank. Get hold of yourself." His arm went around my shoulder and I huddled against him, "Take it easy—wash your face and come on down."

It was about Dianne—father had something to tell us. We faced him in the living room. He closed its doors.

"Sit down, lads."

It may have been in Drake's thoughts, certainly it was in mine, that now father was about to blame us. I had felt, those hours sobbing on the bed, that somehow I was to blame. That incident in the water when I had annoyed Dianne about her hair—wild thoughts swept me that I had annoyed her and she had committed suicide. I had already told father about it; told him in the launch. He had listened and waved it away.

He sat facing us now, a slender, solemn man of fifty, with iron-gray hair, and thin, studious face. His eyes behind his big horn-rimmed spectacles seemed unnaturally bright, but gentle.

He said, "Don't look at me like that, lads—I've no intention of reproaching you."

And then he told us, in a burst, without preface, what we had never suspected.

"You were about two years old, Frank—and you, Drake, about eight. It was the year before your mother died. She and I went to Bird's Nest Island, leaving you children at home."

This same island!

"A summer day," he said, "just about like this. We went for a picnic—just as you did today. It was fifteen years ago. We were wandering about the little island—your mother and I. We heard a wailing cry, an infant's. In a thicket we found a little girl baby. Unharmed. An infant, about a year old, who evidently had been asleep and now had awakened and was crying. There was no boat in sight about this island. We concluded that someone had been there, abandoned the baby and departed. We took the baby home. No one ever came to claim her. It was Dianne."

Dianne not our blood sister? A foundling! It struck us amazed.

Father went on gently, "We thought it best, your mother and I, not to tell you children. It would not have been fair to Dianne. There would come a time when you should know, of course—perhaps I should have told you before this—and I don't know, perhaps it was wrong of me to let you go back to that island. But I suppose that's foolish!"

His voice drifted away with his thoughts. Nothing occurred to Drake and me to say; we sat dumbly staring at each other.

Father rose presently and unlocked a drawer of his desk. "I brought this down to show you. There was nothing about the infant to give a clue to its identity. Just the baby lying there, clad in a single garment. This."

He held out a tiny infant robe. Long-sleeved, and with a tiny hood. Strange-looking thing! Even as a lad of seventeen I was at once aware of its strangeness. A gossamer fabric like nothing I had ever seen before. A fabric golden as though its threads were pale spun gold. Or as though it might have been woven of fairy threads of golden hair—like Dianne's.

"Just that robe," he said sadly. "What sort of material it is, no one can say." He took it from us gently and replaced it in the drawer. "And there was one other thing. You, Frank, spoke of Dianne being sensitive about the hair at her forehead. That little peak where the hair grew low, you remember? There was a scar on her forehead. Not exactly a scar—an odd crescent patch of skin. It seemed not white, but almost like the sheen of silver. It looked—well, something like a crescent moon. We hated publicity, your mother and I. We kept the finding of the baby reasonably quiet. We had a medical specialist examine the child. A normal girl baby, promising extreme beauty of body and feature. But the crescent-moon scar was an enigma—the doctor had never seen or heard of anything like it.

"So we called the baby Dianne. Your mother named her that. The crescent, there on her forehead, was really very beautiful when one got used to it. But too unusual. Too—mysterious. And so we trained her hair to cover it up; and I—I taught her—well, perhaps I taught her to be ashamed of it. Or at least, never to mention it to anyone—and so she was sensitive about it as though it were a secret blemish to her beauty."

I need not detail that evening with father. But there was one thing he said that I never forgot. He said it half to himself, "Dianne was so abnormally beautiful, and that strange golden dress and the crescent silver scar—I have wondered so many times, all these years, wondered if she were just exactly human like the rest of us." He was sorry at once that he had said it, and he would never explain.

This day that we lost Dianne was five years before the coming of the giants.

CHAPTER 1

THE COMING OF THE GIANTS

The first of the giants was reported by a small steamship out of Halifax, bound for Portland. The ship had rounded Cape Sable, Nova Scotia, during the night of March 20th. The sea was stormy; the night overcast with almost a gale from the north. The ship's lookout saw what at first looked like a huge dark rock looming out of the ocean where no rock should have been. It was well inshore from the ship; and though it was only a few miles away, it was not seen clearly.

The ship continued on her course. An hour later, the full moon broke through a rift in the clouds, painting the sullen sea with silver. To the north, where the southern headlands of the land were barely visible, a giant human figure was seen standing in the ocean. Every one on the ship saw it clearly. Incredible as the vision of a fabled sea monster, yet there it was, unmistakable, frightening—it threw the ship's company into a panic of terror.

The thing seemed human. The giant figure of a man. He stood waist-deep in the ocean with the waves beating against his naked chest. How deep the water was, the master of the ship could not say. Ten fathoms perhaps, in the shallows where the giant stood—sixty feet; and his torso towered another sixty above the surface. He stood watching the ship. Then, as it passed, he followed it; wading slowly along to keep abreast of it as doubtless he had been doing for an hour past. In the moonlight, details were plain. A bullet-headed giant. Some said that they could see his features—human of cast, but brutish.

The figure kept its distance, regarding the ship, but making no effort to approach. The vessel turned in a moment off its course, and fled south. The moon was presently obscured. They saw no more of the giant.

This steamship carried wireless. But the master could see no rational way of sending such a wild report. But when hours later, the vessel docked in Portland, the tale was given out.

In these days of skeptical enlightened civilization one cannot claim to have seen a sea serpent and expect anything but laughter. And this was even more incredible. The ship's commander, within a few hours, even doubted the evidence of his own senses. But from the sailors the tale leaked out. And a whole ship's company cannot be insane, or all similarly drunk at once.

The newspapers caught at it, and spread it jocularly until the officials of the freight line cursed their captain and all the crew of the ship for arousing such ridicule.

But still there was some corroboration. From a village near Cape Sable came the report that a giant man had been seen wading in the ocean, seen by a few people during a brief period of moonlight, and then was gone.

Where the figure came from, or where it went, none could say. It was seen just this one night. The tale went around the world and caused a smile, and in a few days was forgotten.

That was the first of the giants.

I was at this time a pilot in the International Mail Service, flying a local plane from Boston up the coast to St. John, daytimes. Up one day with several stops along the route; and back the next day; and then a day off duty. Drake had become father's assistant. They had a laboratory in New York City, and were living now in our Westchester home. Our home on the Maine shore was closed for the winter.

Once a week I went to New York to be with father and Drake. I got there the day the giant was reported. It was of particular interest to me, since it was not far from my flying route.

Father said, "You keep your eyes open, Frank. And look here, if you see anything—don't report it at once. Telephone me."

He was so solemn that I laughed. And Drake was solemn, too.

I demanded, "I say, you two—you don't believe this fool thing, do you?"

"Perhaps," said Drake.

I think that even then they had some vague idea of what it might mean. I thought the yarn was absurd; still less could I have imagined our own connection with it. Never once did I link it with Dianne. It was nearly five years now since that day she had vanished.

I made my next northward flight with no sign of a giant. Nor did I see anything unusual upon the return. In a few days more, like the rest of the world, I had lost interest.

Then one day near the end of March when I was off duty in Boston, another giant was reported. It had been seen the preceding night. A giant man—fifty feet tall, or three hundred, according to the differing, confused versions. The figure had appeared in the ocean, possibly near the mouth of the Penobscot River in northern Maine. Several coast villages and several ships reported seeing the figure, wading north a mile offshore. It was reported almost all the way to the Bay of Fundy. And then it vanished.

This was too obvious for disbelief. No damage had been done. The thing apparently had encountered no ships; it had nowhere come ashore. But the sea was calm this night; the waves of the wading figure had rolled in and pounded the coast to give tangible evidence that the thing was no vision.

The world was more than interested this time. There were near-panics in Boston that day—an exodus of people leaving the city by rail and by airplanes. Several of the local ships from New York to Boston canceled their sailings. People began leaving Cape Cod. There was disorganization, almost a flight from all the cities and villages up the coast.

This was far different from some understood danger. A hurricane, a volcano, an earthquake—people will often face them with a stoicism amounting to foolhardiness, rather than abandon their homes. But this was the unknown, the supernatural. A gruesome horror. Within a day military law was declared all up the Maine coast. Troops were patrolling the area, and the people were being urged to leave.

My chief sent for me at field headquarters. My mate was there; and the two alternate pilots of the route.

"We've discontinued temporarily," he told us. He turned to me as the senior pilot. "Ferrule, the government wants this area patrolled by plane at night. Boston to the New Brunswick border, to connect with Canadian patrol planes. You and Jones want to tackle it?"

We did, of course. We were dispatched that same night—one of six or eight planes flying independently of one another. We left Boston about ten that evening, I and my relief pilot, Bob Jones; and we carried a newly installed code radio with a fellow named Green to operate it.

It is a run of about three hundred miles from Boston, up the crescent curve of coast to the Canadian border. Our orders were to fly at about a thousand feet of altitude, keeping a mile or so offshore. If we saw one of these giants we were to follow it, keep it in sight, and try to determine where it went. We were to report at once by radio. A battleship had already been ordered north; it was to remain in Cape Cod waters, waiting further developments.

The night was calm and starlit. An hour passed. Then two hours. We saw nothing unusual. We were up around the Penobscot now.

Jones, at my elbow, murmured, "One was seen here, Frank. That last one—"

A plane came by, flying south. Another patrol doubtless. We felt that no giant could be ahead of us or this other plane would have seen him; stopped and stayed with him.

The flattened moon came up out of the sea to the east. It was golden at first, laying a broad golden path on the water.

We passed over the many islands. We saw a ship or two—and occasionally a plane.

And then we saw the giant! The actual sight of him, even fortified by what I expected, was a shock of horror.

Jones murmured, "Good God!" He gripped my arm impulsively, but I shook him off.

"Don't do that, you fool!"

"Look at him, Frank!" Bob cried then.

He was no more than a mile or so ahead. He stood at the entrance to a cove. A rocky headland perhaps a hundred feet high was beside him; and he stood with a hand resting against it as though to steady himself. The ocean surface lapped at his knees.

To the right, a mile or so offshore, was the tiny dark blob of an island. Bird's Nest Island! I realized it suddenly. And this was our cove. Our summer home was set in the trees only a few hundred yards back from where the giant was standing.

Green's radio was sending the news. He hunched down, intent at his work. Jones was shaking beside me.

"Lower, Frank! Get down near him!"

We spiraled down. The moonlight was on him, a hundred-foot figure of a man, naked from the waist up. He had pale hair, close cut, on a round head.

"Frank, look at the people!"

A group of tiny black figures was on the cliff, standing in fascinated horror. The giant had not moved; and then with a swift step and a flip of his arm he reached back over the cliff. The tiny figures were scattered. In a patch of moonlit rock two of them lay dead.

We passed only a few hundred feet above the giant. He looked up as though confused or annoyed at the sound of our motors.

Green cautioned me: "Not too close, Frank! If he ever reached—"

That giant hand could have knocked us down into the sea as though we had been a tiny humming insect.

We circled, zoomed up a trifle, and came back. The news had spread. There were two other planes here with us now. A confusion was on shore. We could see, far back, figures and vehicles moving in the moonlight. And lights. And far out to sea, there were the lights of a ship.

We passed again over the giant. Another plane arrived. Four of us, buzzing like insects over the monstrous figure. It turned suddenly and began wading out to sea.

Jones cried: "Look! He's smaller! By George, he is smaller!"

The figure did seem less gigantic. Or perhaps it was the deeper water around him. Then suddenly he sank prone and was swimming. The sea was lashed white with his strokes. Swimming for Bird's Nest Island? It seemed so.

"Lower, Frank! Take us down!"

"Not too close," cautioned Green, for fear he'd stand up again suddenly.

We swept under another plane. The swimming giant flung up an arm; a surge of the water mounted like a geyser in the moonlight. His flashing arms and the black blob of his head were visible. He was halfway to the island. Was he still smaller now?

Then suddenly he dived. The ocean closed over him. The waves he had made rolled away. The surface was calm, unbroken. We waited. Minutes. He did not come up.

The other planes with us swept back and forth, dangerously close to the surface at times. But the giant was gone. We waited half an hour. We crossed over Bird's Nest Island several times. Its tiny rocky peak stood naked in the brilliant moonlight; its trees and shrubbery were deep green; its beach shone clear with the moonlight on it and the calm sea rolling up.

No sign of the giant. And then we were ordered to return to Boston. We turned south.

We were an hour on our southern flight when Green picked up our call. A message for me.

"Your father, Ferrule—he's sent word through headquarters. We're ordered to land at Bennett Field, New York, so you can go to your father and your brother Drake at once." He added: "The exact message—personal, you'll probably understand it—your father says tell you to come at once. He has heard from Dianne."

CHAPTER 2

THE MYSTERIOUS VISITOR

This same night that I was flying the patrol, father and Drake spent at our home in a small Westchester town near New York. They knew in what I was engaged. They were frequently connected by telephone with the official Boston station to which Green was making our radio reports.

Our Westchester home was an unpretentious cottage, set on a quiet street near the edge of the village. We kept only one servant. She was away this night; Drake and father were alone in the house.

There came, just before midnight, a thumping on the front porch door.

They looked up, startled. The thump was repeated. Some one at the front door, demanding admittance.

"Well," said Drake, "it's a wonder they wouldn't ring the bell! I'll go, father."

We had an electric front doorbell, with the button prominently displayed. And also, on the door for ornament, an old-fashioned knocker. This summons was not even a knock; a thump, as though someone were pounding with the flat of his fist. It began again and continued.

"What the deuce?" Drake muttered. He lighted the hall light; father followed him. Drake, with his six feet two inches of brawn, was, at the age of twenty-eight, afraid of no man. But a vague thrill of fear shot through him nevertheless as he went to the door and jerked it open.

A man stood there; a tall, bulky figure, though not so tall as Drake—a man in a long, dark overcoat, with a black felt hat pulled down over his eyes. At first glance he was a rough-looking customer.

"What do you want?" Drake demanded. "We've got a doorbell."

"Does it—is Dr. Ferrule who lives here?" A soft voice; the accent of a foreigner. But Drake could not place the nationality; the voice and broken accent were like nothing he had ever heard before. The light fell on the man's face, heavy-jawed, hairless. A man of perhaps thirty-five.

"Yes," said Drake. "Dr. Ferrule is here." Father was behind him. "For you, father."

The man stood at the threshold. "Then you are Drake Ferrule? Is that true?"

Father advanced. "Come in. What is it? You want to see me? I am Dr. Ferrule."

The man came in. Though the door opening was two feet higher than his head, nevertheless he stooped as he passed it. He stood in the hall.

"Dr. Ferrule, I would like to speak to you—and to this your son. This is Drake?"

Drake said impatiently: "That's my name. Who are you? What do you want?"

The visitor addressed father. "My name? You never heard it. My business? You had a daughter—"

That electrified them. Drake caught father's warning glance and remained silent. Father was trembling. "My daughter—Dianne?"

"Yes, Dianne."

"Come in," said father. He led the man to the library. Drake followed behind, watchfully. He somehow sensed that this mysterious visitor was no friend. An antagonist of some sort. In the library the fellow stood with his hat on. He pushed back its brim as though it annoyed him. He stood ill at ease; his gaze roved the room. To Drake, watching him closely, it seemed that he was somehow expectant; and tense, afraid perhaps of something which might at any moment occur.

"Sit down," said father.

He was more than mysterious, this visitor. Weird. He stood carefully watching father sit down. Then he drew a chair forward and awkwardly sat upon it. As though he had never seen a chair before. The thought flashed to Drake.

"Well?" said father.

There was a brief silence. Drake remained standing. Father, by temperament nervous, was visibly trembling. But he was no fool; he was very cautious, alert.

"Well, what is it? About my daughter Dianne."

"Yes. She—you have not seen her for many years?"

"No."

"Not even heard from her?"

"No. Why?"

It seemed to have been an important question to the visitor. The shadow of a triumphant smile came to his face. He said: "When you last saw her—I understand that you lived on the Maine coast, Dr. Ferrule. But I find you here now in New York—"

"Who the devil are you?" Drake put in.

"Wait, Drake! We live in Maine in the summer," said father. "What is it you have to tell me?"

"I came," he said, "to warn you." The fellow's voice and words, for all his awkward manner, were perfectly composed. He had, even, a strange sort of dominance, as though in his own environment he were accustomed to command. His hat seemed to continue to annoy him. He took it off. He had a massive bullet head, with pale-gold hair close-clipped. Slate-blue eyes; a high-bridged nose. A solidly square chin. Strange, massive face! Strangely forceful, and, Drake thought, strangely evil. The thin lips curved into a smile.

"I came," he repeated, "to warn you. I hear there are giants up near your summer home."

Father said, more vehemently than he had spoken before: "What about them? Do you know where they come from? Look here, hadn't you better tell us who you are? You act very strange."

The man abruptly stood up. "I will go now."

It was too much for Drake. "The hell you will! Not till you've told us your business! You come here, question us, and go—"

He seemed not disturbed by Drake's attack. "You excite yourself, young fellow. Dr. Ferrule, I would suggest it, you stay away from your house up there in Maine."

"Thank you," said father, with his quiet irony. "Drake, wait a minute!"

"Stay away because—there might be danger there for you."

"From what?" Drake demanded.

"From the giants."

"What about them? You know anything about them?"

He gestured deprecatingly. "No more than you. But I would say it, they must be dangerous."

The fellow was trying to withdraw. He moved toward the door. Whatever the purpose of his visit, he seemed to have accomplished it.

Father and Drake followed him. At the library doorway instinctively he stooped again. He had put on his hat. Drake noticed that he had it on backward.

In the hall father said: "Is this all you've got to say?"

"Yes."

"You—you mentioned my daughter."

He did not answer. He waited until the front door of the house was open. He kept away from Drake. Then he said abruptly: "You will never see Dianne again. Forget her."

He half ran, half leaped across the porch; leaped its steps, and darted away.

Drake started in pursuit, but father called him back.

The running figure was in a moment lost in the shadows of the dark street.

CHAPTER 3

THE SIGNAL FIRE

Some six hours later, in the early morning, I arrived. Father and Drake had not been to bed. They described the mysterious midnight visitor. I could make little of it, save that Dianne was alive. Had this fellow abducted her? Was he holding her? Had he come to sound out whether father would pay a ransom?

Father waved away my theories. He was visibly shaken. There was one thing upon which he and Drake were agreed. The visitor had been wholly strange. Something about him almost uncanny.

Father said slowly: "We don't know what it means. That fellow last night—he came, we think, just to find out if Dianne were with us. Something he said, or the way he said it, gave us that impression. It seems possible that he knew Dianne is trying to rejoin us. It may be that he is an enemy of Dianne's. I think—wherever Dianne is—she may be trying to get to us. We must help her do that."

"But how?" I demanded.

Drake said: "She might try to get back to our place, up there in Maine. We feel we should be there now, Frank. That fellow last night—damn fool!—thought he could keep us from going there by warning us away!"

"But who was he?" I insisted. My mind was groping with vague ideas—like father's and Drake's perhaps; ideas too fantastic for discussion. "What has your visitor got to do with us? Or Dianne? Or these giants? I don't see the connection, but there is one, that's obvious."

Father said very slowly: "You, Frank, seemed to think that giant you saw last night was changing size—dwindling. Perhaps while he was under the water he grew so small that when he came up you did not see him. Don't ask us what it means! We don't know. But I really think that fellow who called upon Drake and me last night was one of the giants!"

We left New York that same morning in an official plane which dropped us in the afternoon near our home in Maine. What father told the authorities I do not know. He said he told them as little as possible. Whatever our connection with this affair, for Dianne's sake it seemed best not to make it public. But father got me leave of absence from my flying duties, and secured us an official plane, and a permit for us to live in our Maine home, within the threatened area which now was completely under military rule.

It was mid-afternoon when by automobile we reached our house. We had been stopped half a dozen times by State troops patrolling all the roads leading to the coast. One officer chanced to know father.

"It's risky, Dr. Ferrule. You know what you're doing, of course. But down there—your isolated house right on the shore—"

"We know what we're doing," said father.

I put in: "Shucks, there's no danger. Might never have another giant appear."

The town of Elton, two miles from our home, looked as though it were in a state of siege. Half its people had fled. Troops patrolled the streets. Many of the houses were closed and barred—as though that would help against a hundred-foot giant! The shops were nearly all closed; but we located several of the owners and loaded our car with provisions.

On arriving, father went to bed. He was never in robust health, and the nervous excitement of all this and his loss of sleep had about done him up. He was too tired to eat the meal which Drake and I hastily prepared. But he was a fighter, every inch of him. He lay down, fully dressed, with an automatic beside his pillow.

"You lads can stand guard—suit yourselves—only don't both sleep at once. Call me if anything unusual happens."

Drake and I sat on guard. We were neither of us sleepy. It seemed as though there were a thousand things we wanted to talk about, but it was all so intangible. We were in what undoubtedly was the heart of the threatened area. The world believed that; and no one knew it better than ourselves.

We had had the latest official reports. No other giant was seen. There had been several people killed by a sweep of the giant's arm last night, quite near here on the cliff top. Official searching parties had been over every inch of Bird's Nest Island and all the shore in this vicinity. Nothing unusual was found. They had even dragged the water between here and the island, thinking perhaps the giant's body might have sunk.

There were other reports which now had come in. Gruesome things! In the back country near here a farmer had been found dead a few nights ago, and all his clothes stolen. There were several similar incidents.

At sunset a destroyer steamed past, headed north on patrol. There were often airplanes passing overhead. And out at sea there was a smudge which we thought might be a battleship.

With darkness came a sense of loneliness—the feeling of our isolation here in this house set close against the coast. We were in danger here, but not altogether foolhardy. We had rifles and several automatics. And the telephone would at any time bring us help from the troops stationed in the nearby village.

To fight what? It would all be so useless against a hundred-foot giant!

The vigil grew irksome. Would Dianne come? How? When? Tonight? Tomorrow? A week or a month from now—or never? They were such futile questions. And it seemed, as we sat there on guard, that we might be menaced not only by giants. There was father's midnight visitor in New York, just last night. Was he—or others like him—lurking about our place here? We sat, often straining our ears for every sound outside the house.

Father slept soundly. The evening passed. It was a dark night; a few moving lights out at sea. We saw nothing unusual, heard nothing.

Midnight came. "You better go to sleep," Drake said, when we had rustled up another meal. "I'll sit here till dawn, then call you. We'll have to get some regular schedule."

Sleep was a long time coming. Then I slept dreamlessly, to be awakened by Drake pulling at me.

"It will soon be daylight, Frank."

I leaped up. "Nothing happened?"

"No."

"How's father?"

"All right. Still pounding it out. He was awake with me for an hour or two. Then I made him go back. The fire's going in the living room, Frank. There's a pot of coffee on the hearth if you want it. Here, want this automatic?"

"No. I've got mine."

He lay down with his weapon beside him, and I left him. I went out into the living room. Its oil lamp was burning. In the big open fireplace a log fire was going with a pot of coffee on the hearth. I had my automatic in my pocket; beside the hearth three loaded rifles and a shotgun were standing.

Through the windows to the east I could see that the stars were paling.

* * * *

The dawn came. The room brightened with its flat light. I put out the lamp. The fire burned low.

It was now broad daylight. A clear, crisp morning. Silent and still; not a breath of wind. Drake had been asleep perhaps two hours. I went again to the veranda. There were no planes, no boats in sight, except out at sea where the warship still hovered.

Bird's Nest Island stood clear in the morning sunlight. From the island a wisp of smoke was rising. Some one there—a camp fire. Soldiers, perhaps.

I stood gazing. The smoke rose in a thin, dark wisp, straight up into the still air. Then suddenly the column broke. The smoke was checked. And in a moment it came again. A dark, round puff of it rising. Then another puff. And others. As though a blanket were being held over a smoking fire, to catch the smoke, releasing it in puffs.

A stream of them now. Two large ones. Three, smaller. Two large ones again.

A signal fire? But it was not only that thought which made my heart pound. I recognized the signal! My mind flung back to childhood days. Myself, Dianne and Drake. Fanciful children out on this same island; building a camp fire; making the smoke signals as we thought Robinson Crusoe might have done. Two large puffs; then three smaller. This was our childish signal, out there now!

CHAPTER 4

THE STRANGE ISLAND

"Drake! Wake up!"

I routed him out hastily. The signal was still showing. Drake remembered it, just as I did. We watched it; and after a moment it ceased. The wisp of smoke went up unbroken; and then presently it dissipated and vanished.

We stared at each other.

"You think it's Dianne?" I asked.

"Yes. It might be." He was confused. "I don't know what to think, Frank. We must go there—get over there quickly as we can—see what it means."

"Yes," I agreed. "I wonder if our dory is down at the boathouse. You mean, row over? I don't think father will want to say anything at the village; get a launch? Do you?"

"No." We both felt, as we knew father did, a reticence against taking the authorities into our confidence. If Dianne came—to have an official investigation of her, with all the publicity—it was unthinkable.

"Let's see about the dory," Drake suggested.

"Shall we wake father up?"

"Let's see about the dory first."

We found the dory safe in the boathouse.

We decided to start at once. A row of half an hour. We went to awaken father.

"Think he'll want to come with us, Drake?"

"He might—I hope he'll stay here. This might just be a coincidence—not Dianne. We should not all leave here at once, Frank."

"Why not?"

He stopped and faced me. "Because suppose she—appeared while we were gone?"

Appeared? He said it with a hitch in his voice. As though Dianne might materialize from nothing into solidity before us! Yet we both felt like that. This whole affair seemed supernatural.

"Yes," I said. "That's true."

And father felt the same. He decided to stay on guard. He made us take two automatics, and a rifle in the bottom of the dory. He was refreshed from his sleep. Alert and vigorous.

"I'll be all right, lads." He followed us down to the boathouse. He was white and grim as he said, "I need not tell you to be cautious. Come back quickly as you can."

We launched the dory and headed into the cove. He called, "If I don't see you starting back in two hours I'll bring a launch after you."

Drake and I hardly spoke during the trip. The rifle lay at Drake's feet; we had our automatics strapped to our belts. We stripped off our coats for the work of rowing. In the stern we had other coats—oilskins, which always were kept in the dory.

We approached the island. Drake eased up. "Wait a minute—let's see if anybody shows."

The smoke had long since vanished. We could not be sure at what part of the island the fire had been. There was no sign of it now. The little island stood green in the morning sunlight, with the peak of rock looming at its center. The beach on this side was empty; there was no evidence of any living thing there, save a few gulls lazily circling overhead.

We were armed, and this was broad daylight. But the thought of that strange midnight visitor swept me. I know Drake felt the same as we pulled up in the sunlight of the island beach. We were not afraid of anything human.

Drake carried the rifle. I had my automatic out. We started off down the silent beach. Rounded its end. All empty. We kept near the water, away from the trees and underbrush.

No sign of anything. Drake whispered. "Let's cut straight across. Then up to the rock. Look for the fire embers."

He led us, with the rifle in the hollow of his arm. We walked slowly, cautiously through the trees as though stalking some hidden animal.

But there seemed no one on the island.

Drake called suddenly, "Dianne! Oh, Dianne!"

It startled me; it echoed through the silent trees. We stood listening. Nothing.

We went on again. We came to the opposite beach. Drake whispered, "The fire must have been to the south."

We went that way. Back from the shore, some fifty feet from the beach we came upon the embers of a small fire. They were still faintly smoking.

No one here. We stood in this little glade, our gazes roving.

Nothing here. Just a few embers and half-burned sticks. I bent down.

"Water was thrown on the fire to put it out," I said softly. "These sticks are wet."

I was on one knee. My heart leaped into my throat. There was a patch of grass and ferns near me. Something stirred in them. A bird moving through the grass? But it was not that. I stared.

A fern not much higher than my ankle moved and bent aside.

My breath stopped. I stared, unbelieving. And Drake saw it. He muttered something and took a backward step.

The fern leaf moved further. A tiny figure, no taller than the blades of grass around it, was disclosed. A human figure an inch or so high!

And there were others, lurking in the grass. One came out. The figure of a woman the height of my finger. A woman with long golden robe. Pale-gold hair dangling. The tiny face stared up at me, only a few feet away as I knelt. A face the size of my finger nail! The sunlight fell on it. A girl, humanly beautiful. Small and colorful, this living face, as a miniature painted on ivory.

And I recognized it. I gasped. "Dianne, it's you!"

CHAPTER 5

PRINCESS OF THE ATOM

Drake and I were transfixed; amazed, doubting the evidence of our senses. Yet there was Dianne at our feet. She stood with a hand holding a fern stalk. Her little face was smiling. I heard a voice, of microscopic smallness, but clear. Dianne's voice; her familiar accents.

"You came, Frank. I—we've been waiting."

I became aware that Drake had taken a step or two forward. The little figures in the grass scattered. Dianne called up sharply, "Careful, Drake! Don't step on us! Stand quiet! In a moment I'll be larger."

She turned and ran into the grass. Its blades were no higher than the length of my hand, but as though they were a jungle of huge green stalks they sheltered the small human figures. Half a dozen men, and one other girl, like Dianne, but with a robe of pale silvery white.

The figures clustered together. We could hear their faint voices. Words in a language unintelligible. Then the two girls drew apart. The men moved away. Hiding, watching from the concealing grass.

Amazing sight! Inconceivable shock to our normal senses! Before our eyes, Dianne and this other girl were becoming larger. A visible change. In a moment they were above the grass. They moved away from it. They bent the ferns aside. Dianne trampled one now. They came out into the little open patch of rock and pebbles where Drake and I were standing by the embers of the camp fire. Already they were as tall as our knees.

Dianne's voice, now more familiar than ever, said, "Don't look like that! Move back. Don't stand so close to us!"

For a moment neither Drake nor I spoke. A new realization of this thing swept me. The menacing giants along the coast had disappeared because they had become small. I had already contemplated that. But I had envisaged them only as small as myself. Like the midnight visitor who had called upon Drake and father. Yet here were humans still smaller.

And I realized then that what we had called a giant could be lurking here upon this island now. Any of these little patches of grass would shelter him, and a thousand like him.

Dianne had been furtive with her smoke signal to us. She had made it; and then had grown small with her companions, to hide in the grass and await our coming. She was so obviously furtive! As tall as my waist now, she gazed around anxiously as though, with her greater height than before, she might now discern some near-by enemy.

The girl with her seemed equally apprehensive. An air of haste enveloped them both.

And I saw now that the tiny figures of the men in the grass were spreading out and vanishing. Or searching? Or guarding? Their smallness making it possible for them to seek out any lurking tiny enemies which to us in our gigantic size could never be found.

A minute or two only while my thoughts roved and I clung to Drake and stared at Dianne and this strange girl growing large before us; Dianne, every minute as she neared what to me was her normal size, becoming more familiar of aspect.

The same Dianne—our little sister! Yet how different! The long golden robe was of that same strange fabric as the infant dress father had shown us in which she had been found. Her pale-gold hair flowed free to her waist. But it did not come down into a peak on her forehead now. It was drawn back; and there on her forehead was the silver crescent patch. It seemed to glow. Unnatural. Uncanny. Yet it was a thing beautiful. It blended with her beauty. And it made her seem strangely regal.

She said abruptly, "Ahlma—enough!"

The hand of each of the girls went suddenly to their mouths. They reeled, clutching at each other; and Drake and I, with recovered wits, moved to aid them. But they steadied. They smiled. And they had stopped growing. Dianne, about as tall as I had always remembered her; this other girl, whom she had called Ahlma, a trifle taller; and it seemed, perhaps, a year or two older. A girl singularly beautiful in Dianne's own fashion. Golden hair like Dianne's. And a crescent on her forehead. But it seemed a paler crescent than Dianne's.

Drake stammered, "Why, Dianne!"

I think he had said that and nothing else half a dozen times before.

The girls were still furtive, apprehensive. Dianne said hurriedly, "Don't question now, Drake. Frank, dear—stop looking at me like that! Your boat is here?"

I said, "Yes, Dianne."

"This is Ahlma. My servant and my friend. Is father all right, Frank?"

"Yes."

"I want to get to him. Take us to the boat. Have you something you can cover us with?"

Her hand gripped my arm. It strangely reassured me to feel her human grip. Drake reached out hesitantly and touched her. And she laughed and kissed us both. Our same human, beautiful little Dianne.

"Ahlma, these all my life were my brothers."

"We have coats in the boat," I said.

"Is father here? At the house here?"

"Yes," said Drake. "Come."

We started with them for the boat.

"You're afraid," said Drake. "You have enemies here? These giants?"

"But I can't tell you now! Yes, enemies. They know what I am trying to do. They want to stop me. One of them, the leader—we call him Togaro—"

She gazed around us. "He is here, I think. He and a party of his men. Drake, you can't realize the jungle deeps of this vast island when you are small! Deserts of rock—vast caverns—it's so different when you are small! I'm afraid of him—I want to get to father."

We came to the beach. She added, "I would tell you now what I have come for. But he might be here at our feet. He knows, I think, that I have come to join you."

The midnight visitor. Was he this Togaro?

"Get in," said Drake. He stared at the girl in the white robe. He said to her, "This thing is so inconceivably strange to us—we don't know what to say—we—am I to call you Ahlma?"

She met his gaze and smiled; and it seemed that a faint wave of color suffused her neck and face. She said, with an odd accent. "Yes, I am Ahlma. You are Drake—and you are Frank. I have heard very much from Dianne about you."

Her voice gave Drake a startled realization. Her accent was indescribable. But Drake recognized it! Unmistakably the accent of the midnight visitor.

The girls sat in the stern of the dory. We covered them with the oilskins so that anyone observing us would see nothing unusual about them.

They had searched and made us search the boat. There was no human thing aboard it save ourselves. No figure even the size of our finger could have lurked there and escaped our search.

But as we rowed from the island, Dianne's fear did not lessen. She said, "We've done the best we could. If they are here—"

She did not finish. She added, "You haven't told anyone—no one—I mean the authorities—knows about me?"

"No, Dianne."

"Because, what I want you to do—you and father—it must be secret. And Togaro, he will prevent your doing it if he can."

Strange words! She would not add to them. She sat silent and tense as we rowed across the sunlit channel, and brought her home, where father was waiting for us.

* * * *

"I'll tell them," said father. "Come in lads. We must be brief, Dianne. You're right that haste is necessary."

Father had been with Dianne and her strange girl companion for perhaps half an hour. He called us in at last. He sat with his arm about Dianne. I could see at once that he was tense and grim; and the apprehension characteristic of Dianne lay now upon him also.

His quick glances about the room—as though he were trying to see the unseeable. This thing uncanny—I saw too, that the room's windows were carefully closed; and the heavy shades drawn, so that for all the daylight outside, a lighted lamp was needed. Father told us sharply to close the door after us.

He said, as we sat down:

"I was right to insist upon talking to Dianne alone. There are things I could understand better than you—we have no time for discussion."

I burst out: "Are you going to keep on treating us like children?"

"No. Frank. You have a right to know these strange things Dianne has told me. But we have no time for argument." His voice was low. He spoke swiftly, with what seemed a surreptitious haste.

The girl Ahlma sat apart. Her gaze roved the room, especially the floor.

She said abruptly, "Dianne, can we not close up the bottom of that door?"

There was perhaps a quarter of an inch space between the bottom of the door and the sill. Father got up and kicked a rug against the door. He turned up the wick of the lamp so that the room was brighter.

"Will that do?"

"Yes," said Dianne. "That's better."

Drake and I stared at each other. Drake wet his lips, but did not speak. This thing was ghastly.

Father said abruptly, "Dianne was born, not in this world of ours, but in a world infinitely small. A world within an atom of rock, there on Bird's Nest Island—a world of humans like ourselves.

"Like us? Why, you can see for yourselves! Dianne was born a princess of the civilization on one of the globes whirling in the limitless space within that atom.

"I confuse you, lads? I am talking of infinite smallness. There is no limit to smallness. We know that. But I can't go into such a subject now."

"Afterward, you can tell them," said Dianne with her gentle smile. "All I have told you—time then, father."

"You still call me father?" he said. "So strange, these things."

Drake said, "Dianne was brought here when she was a baby. Why?"

"A princess," father repeated. "And soon after she was born an evil leader came into power in her world. Human life is the same everywhere, lads. She has told me it all—you shall hear every detail. But now—I need tell you only that Dianne's parents, with their throne threatened, had their scientists spirit Dianne away. They have a drug—you can call it that—and a space-flying vehicle, capable of changing size. They brought their little princess out into what to them is infinite largeness. Left her here. To save her life from this conqueror who threatened their throne."

My thoughts reached to grasp what father was saying. I could envisage an atom of rock there on Bird's Nest Island. One atom out of the uncounted billions. It chanced to contain human life. I tried to imagine becoming infinitely small. Space would, by comparison, open up around me. The whirling electrons within the atom would be blazing suns in a firmament of illimitable space. With a space-flying vehicle infinitely small, I could then traverse that starry universe. Land upon a dark star—a planet—an earth. And find there a human civilization.

I knew something of modern physics. I knew that the similarity of atomic structure to our astronomical universe was already recognized. A difference of size only. And all comparative. I could hold a fragment of rock on the palm of my hand. Billions of atoms, clinging together to make what I saw as a tiny rock fragment. Yet each of those atoms held within itself a starry universe of limitless distance—if I were to become small enough to see it from the other viewpoint.

I stared at Dianne. My sister? There suddenly seemed a vast gulf between us. This gentle creature, so strangely beautiful, with the crescent glowing on her forehead. Not my sister. A princess of a different world.

She caught my gaze and smiled. And said, as she had said several times before, "Don't look at me like that, Frank! I'll tell them, father. That day Frank, when you and I and Drake went to the island. You call it five years ago? When you left me, this Togaro suddenly appeared. He took me—into the atom—into smallness—into what soon I learned was my own native world.

"He wanted the throne which some day would have been mine. He—he wanted—he wants me. But the people turned against him. I was rescued—taken from him. I am ruler of that world now. I've told all the details—your father will explain to you."

She was speaking fast, almost breathlessly. And I realized now the regal dominance of her manner, mixed so strangely with the little Dianne we used to know.

She went on: "I've come back here—and Togaro knows it. He learned, some long time ago, our scientists' secret of traveling into largeness—into this world of yours so gigantic. He learned English from me. He learned many things of your Earth and its people.

"He has been here and seen for himself. He is here now—with a few of his men. You have seen some of them. They happened to be a trifle larger than your normal size and so you call them giants."

Drake put in, "Dianne, wait! Can't you answer some questions?"

"I would keep her here with us always," father said. "She knows that. But she is going back at once. Her duty lies in there with her people. But more than that—the menace of Togaro here—she must go back!"

"You don't talk so we can understand you, father," I objected.

The girl Ahlma spoke again. She addressed Dianne, but her gaze was on Drake.

"I think, Dianne, you should tell them at once why we came. What it is they must do for us."

Father said, "Lads, this Togaro and hordes of his followers are planning to come from the atom. Some are already here. That's what Dianne and her people want to stop. For our sake. She wants us to get this atom of rock from Bird's Nest Island. Bring it here. She will go back within it to her world. We are to keep it here. Guard it. You see? Watch it, or have it watched day and night. Then the coming of Togaro's hordes can be checked. We can see them appear—kill them as they come, when still they are tiny."

Dianne interrupted him. "Togaro's plan is to come here—and with his men in a size gigantic even compared to you, he will overrun your Earth! Conquer it! Force your great nations to yield to his giants—"

Giants overrunning our world! I could with shuddering fancy imagine one a thousand feet tall toppling the buildings of New York City with sweeps of his arm! Of what use our battleships, our long-range guns—any of our weapons against a horde of such gigantic antagonists?

Father said, "Our Earth could be devastated so easily! But if we can get the atom here, now before it is too late—"

A cry from Ahlma checked him. There was an instant when all of us sat mute with horror. In a distant corner of the room where a glow of our table light fell upon the floor the small figure of a man was lurking. A man, tall perhaps as the top of my shoe.

An instant while we were mute, frozen into immobility. Then I heard Dianne murmur, "Togaro!"

And Drake cried, "Father—that is the fellow who called on us last night!"

Drake's chair crashed over backward as he leaped to his feet. He stooped. He seized the chair and flung it at the little lurking figure.

I shouted, "You missed him, Drake!" I dashed across the room. I had seen the figure dart into a shadow.

Dianne lifted off the lampshade and tossed it away. The room floor showed more clearly. We hastily moved the furniture. Then I saw the figure again. Far smaller now—an inch high, no more. It had climbed to the baseboard of the wall. Running upon the narrow ledge. It leaped—the shadow of a chair enveloped it.

We ran about the room, searching. Like searching for an insect which every instant was dwindling toward invisibility.

Dianne cried, "Too late! He's too small. But I saw him—right near here."

She gripped me as I passed her. And cried, "Drake, wait! You and Frank, will you come with me? If we get small—follow him into smallness here in this room—we may catch him! Will you come?"

CHAPTER VI

THE CHASE INTO SMALLNESS

Drake and I took the small pellets which Dianne offered. She had them in a phial at her waist. She said hurriedly: "Ahlma, you stay here. Keep her with you, father. Stay here in the room. Watch us—then, when you can't see us any longer, sit down! Don't move about—you might trample on us!"

It seemed that we had last seen the figure along the inner wall, away from the door or the windows. This was a small room. Two windows on one side, and the single door. It had once been a bedroom; but it was furnished meagerly now, with a small table and a few chairs.

"Here," said Dianne, "I think this is the best place. He may be—right here now. He could not go far—not far from this particular spot—when he is so small. Stand beside me, Drake. Here, Frank."

Father stammered: "You—you won't be gone long?"

"No," said Dianne. "Togaro would not dare go far into smallness here. It would lead him into the unknown—he would get lost. We will be back—in an hour perhaps. You ready, Frank? Ready, Drake?"

The pellet tasted a trifle sweetish. It dissolved on my tongue. I gulped and swallowed. Cold beads of sweat stood on my forehead. But it was fear only. My head reeled. The room seemed to take a dizzying, sweeping lurch. Dianne's steadying arm was around me and Drake; and in a moment my senses cleared. I later learned the details of this drug's effect. A contraction of the cells of my body, preserving their form, contracting each of them in normal relation to the others. An aura of its effect, like a magnetic field, was around me. My garments contracting; even the air, as I breathed it, was diminished in all its inherent molecules and atoms.

Dianne's voice said: "You feel all right?"

I heard Drake mutter: "Yes. But—Dianne—strange."

I was standing still, yet everywhere the room was in movement—a crawling, flowing movement. I could see the near-by wall at which I stared, moving upward, expanding, growing steadily larger. The ceiling over me, lifting. The wall receding. A moment ago I could have touched it. Not now. It was drawing back from me. A visual enlargement of all my surroundings. An illusion, because I was dwindling.

I was still dizzy; I did not dare turn my head or shift my gaze. Beside me was a chair. I could see it out of the tail of my eye. The chair was shifting away, and growing huge. Already its seat loomed higher than my head. I saw Dianne and Drake beside me; in all this movement they alone were unchanged.

And I could feel the movement. The floor under my feet was shifting with a steady crawl. It was spreading out, expanding. The pull of it drew my feet apart so that every moment I had to take a step to keep from falling. All this in what perhaps was a minute.

Dianne cast me off. "You're all right now. Come on—I think we should stand nearer the wall."

The wall seemed ten feet or more from us now. We walked toward it. The effect was dizzying, but we overcame that presently. Dianne turned and waved her hand upward. Drake and I swung around to follow her gesture.

This room gigantic! The ceiling seemed thirty or forty feet above us. The opposite wall was farther than that. High up were huge rectangles of windows. The chairs and the table were enormous.

We moved again toward the wall. We ran this time. A foot or two away we stopped.

Another minute passed. The room wall was white plastered, and it had a lower baseboard of wood. The plaster surface rose sheer a hundred feet now. It was like a great cliff-face. The lamplight up there was a yellow glow. The baseboard was twice the height of our heads, with a ledge on top upon which we could have walked. The wood looked rough and jagged.

The visual growth went on. The wall was again far away, and receding so fast that if we ran we might fail to reach it. The board floor under us was turning rough—uneven, with ridges and undulations everywhere.

Another minute.

In the distance behind us one of the table legs rose like a huge monolith into the heights of the lamplight. Shadows and blurred, dark outlines were up there. Farther away on the rolling, jagged surface which was now the floor I could see a formless dark blur which might have been one of father's feet. Half a mile away, perhaps, and receding in the distance.

Then even the nearer wall was gone! Vaguely, as though it were some ten miles off, it loomed like the white sheen of an ice cliff. Then vanished.

We stood alone in the midst of a tumbled region. A great tumbled plain— crudely level. Vacant distance everywhere. Overhead, in what to us was now the sky, a faint yellow sheen of radiance mingled with the haze of space.

There were pits all about us now; depressions, in depth twice the height of our bodies, with steep but jagged sides. We were still diminishing; the landscape crawled with expanding movement. It kept us active now. At our feet, often a small hole would open up so that we would have to move to a higher ridge to keep from falling or sliding into the yawning hole.

We stood precariously upon a small peak. With unnatural microscopic clearness it seemed to me that my vision might carry a hundred miles across this tumbled landscape. Weird vista! Like nothing I had ever seen on earth. Not even like pictures of the lunar landscapes. Some unknown planet, perhaps, might look like this. A land convulsed by an angry nature, flung and tumbled by some great cataclysm into this broken chaos.

With an effort I turned my thoughts into the other viewpoint. This was a few square inches—a foot or two perhaps—of the rough, scuffled board flooring in the bedroom of our Maine home! It seemed, far away as I stared, that there was a great vertical slash crossing the distant horizon. A cañon deep and wide—I knew that probably it was the space between the boards of the floor. A mile or so away in another direction was a huge caldron; a circular pit a mile wide, with a broken and jagged rim. The crater of some volcano? It was in reality a broken knothole, a blemish in the rough board of the floor.

We had been talking at intervals. I said once, thoughtlessly:

"But, Dianne—going into your atom, would it be so very much farther than this?"

She smiled. Drake exclaimed, "Don't be an ass, Frank!"

Dianne said gently, "This would be just the start. I have the drug in a more powerful form."

"How long a trip, Dianne? To get into your world, from ours, I mean?"

"With greater intensities of the drug, Frank, we diminish much faster. The whole trip—you would call it three or four days, perhaps."

Three or four days! And we had been now some five minutes!

We had, all this time, been watching closely for any sign of Togaro. Dianne was sure that he had vanished somewhere near here.

"But, Dianne, when he was larger than we are now," Drake objected, "Why if he ran off there"—he gestured with a sweep of his arm toward our dim horizon—"he'd be a hundred miles from here by now."

She nodded. "Yes. But he would not dare move far. We would see him. But if he were hiding—"

There were certainly places to hide here now. Caverns—yawning tunnel-entrances opening up everywhere.

Dianne cautioned, "Watch out, Frank!"

We had moved down from the ridge; to stay there would have left us stranded upon a precipitous height. Drake and Dianne seized me—I had nearly fallen as the shifting ground altered under me. We clung to a slope; slid down it. We landed, unharmed, some twenty feet down, in a bowl-like depression.

It seemed now that all this area was a honeycomb. Underground passages opened here into the bowl. Tunnels. Caves, small and elongated. All this underground area a honeycomb of cells. Cellular caves of the wood structure!

Drake started thoughtlessly into a dim passageway. But Dianne stopped him.

"We must not separate. If you get lost—"

We stood in a cave. The light was fading. The opening tunnels and expanding pits near us were dark. And it was all very silent. Our voices seemed dead and muffled.

I presently became aware that the expanding movement around us had ceased. The dose of the drug we had taken had reached its limit. We were no longer diminishing.

We stood, instinctively whispering. Was Togaro near here? How in all these miles of cellular caverns could we ever hope to locate him? We walked, keeping close together, through a tubelike passage; came into another cave. We had gone downward; it was even more dim in here.

It occurred to me suddenly that we had brought no weapons. In the awed fear of our taking the drug for the first time, confronting this unknown experience, we had completely forgotten them.

"Could we have brought them?" Drake asked.

"A small revolver perhaps," said Dianne. "Held under your arm. I never thought of it—we have no such weapons in our world. Togaro, I think, will not have them—and you are two against him."

"We'll never find him," I declared. "Not in such a place as this. How small would he get, do you think?"

"He would not dare get very small. It would lead him—you can see—into the unknown."

I could indeed. These caves here under us—another of those pellets; it would carry us down, with illimitable space opening up around us. Even this small area upon which my foot now rested would open up into a universe if I were to get small enough!

Drake said, "No use exploring here. Not in this size. Dianne, how about us getting larger? A trifle larger—and on the upper surface we can move about—cover a greater area. We might locate him—"

Togaro had the drug in the same size pellets as did Dianne. It seemed likely that he would have taken one—come to this size we now had reached. But to go back he would have to get larger again. We might have our best chance of encountering him going back. Or wait, up there in the room—with a bright light and careful watch.

We stood at the entrance of a huge elongated cavern. A dozen of these tunnel mouths, about as high as our heads, opened into it. The cavern was some two hundred feet in length; half as wide and a hundred feet or so high.

A flattened elongated cell. It was dim and shadowed. Our lowered voices reverberated across it with muffled echoes.

Drake said, "No chance this way, Dianne."

But we had miscalculated this fellow Togaro. He had not been attempting to escape us; he was luring us on. Progressively smaller always than ourselves—since he had taken the drug before we did—he had kept within sight of us.

We saw him now, standing along the side of this cavern not fifty feet from us! A stalwart, heavy-set figure; trousers, a white shirt open at the throat exposing a massive hairy chest. He was now somewhat shorter than Drake, though taller than I. He had been lurking in some recess of the cavewall. He came out and the movement attracted us.

I cried, "There he is!"

Drake and I would have rushed at him, but Dianne seized us.

"Wait!"

A glow of light from some overhead opening fell upon the standing figure. Bare-headed; massive, bullet head. A face—the face of the midnight visitor—regarding us sardonically.

And in that instant Drake and I realized why Dianne was holding us. She was fumbling frantically at her belt.

The leering figure of Togaro off there was visibly growing larger! An instant and he was as tall as Drake. Then taller.

He came leaping at us!

CHAPTER 7

THE FLIGHT IN THE CELLULAR CAVERNS

Dianne's hand came from her belt. "Here—take this! Just touch it to your tongue. Only that! Then give it back to me!"

Her hand went to her own mouth. I moistened my tongue with the pellet.

Togaro had almost reached us. Drake leaped forward. Dianne cried in agonized terror, "Oh, Drake—Drake, you took too much!"

Drake had gulped all of his pellet. He leaped at the oncoming figure of Togaro. They locked together, fighting. I broke from Dianne. As I jumped forward a corrugation of the floor caught my foot. I fell headlong; stunned for a moment, but I got up.

In the center of the cavern the swaying forms of Drake and Togaro were fighting. They were both already far larger than Dianne and me! Giant fighting forms. Growing swiftly. In a moment they looked fifteen or twenty feet tall. A weaponless, hand-to-hand fight. Togaro was bending Drake backward. Drake's hands gripped the fellow's throat. Then they went down. Rolling together, each struggling to land on top. Still larger now—their lurching bodies filled one end of the cavern.

Dianne clung to me. I became aware that I was struggling to escape her. And aware also that the cave seemed dwindling. A slow contraction, but the dim space here was already noticeably smaller.

"Dianne, let me go!"

"No! They're too large! You'd be killed!"

Large! They were gigantic! A sweep of one of their massive arms or legs would have flung me headlong as though I had been a child. I crouched with Dianne, watching them. Powerless to help Drake.

Then I realized: "Dianne, give me more of the drug."

"No!" She called, "Drake! Drake, you—"

Her words were lost in the turmoil of the fighting giants. The roof of the cavern had a long irregular opening into the space above it. Light filtered down. The light illumined the huge threshing bodies. Togaro was on top. His arm, longer than my body now, went up as he tried to strike at Drake. Then Drake heaved him off.

They had rolled away from where Dianne and I were crouching. They were soon so large that half the cavern scarce contained them. Togaro tried to stand up with Drake lunging at his waist. His shoulders brushed the roof. He could not stand erect.

Dianne was screaming now. "Drake! Drake! Climb out of here! You'll be crushed!" An agony of fear was in her voice.

It swept me with a realization of horror. Growing so fast, these fighting giants, that in a moment more the cavern would not be large enough for them! Crushed in here by their own growth.

I added my shouts to Dianne's. "Drake! Climb out—through the hole up there."

They both realized the danger. They were almost wedged between this hundred-foot floor and roof. We could see Togaro trying to cast Drake backward—trying to escape through the gash overhead. He seemed to succeed. His fist caught Drake full in the face. Drake crumpled, but in a moment recovered. Togaro had cast loose. Scrambling, half climbing, his great body lurched up through the roof opening.

But Drake was after him. He stood, bent double within the narrow confines of these walls. He scrambled up, against all the efforts of Togaro to shove him back.

They fought in the space over us. Already too large to come back. Their bodies fell as again they locked together. Fell across the roof opening, so huge now that we could see only a portion of their legs.

Again the space up there must have been too small. They scrambled higher. The sounds of the fighting faded into the upper distance.

* * * *

Father sat with Ahlma, watching us as we dwindled before his horrified eyes. He saw us, an inch high, standing by the wall. Dianne called, "Goodby." He saw us smaller, running across the tiny space, still closer to the wall. He did not dare move. He sat by the table with Ahlma beside him. She put her hand out presently and touched his arm; his hand gripped hers and held it.

He said softly, "You love my girl Dianne?"

"Oh, yes. My friend and our princess."

"You're older?"

"A little."

He paused. "Ahlma, will you bring her back to me when this is over? Will you? We'll get the fragment of rock which holds your atom. I'll guard it carefully. Will you bring Dianne back to me?"

She turned her face to him, a face perhaps as beautiful as Dianne's, gentle, thoughtful. She brushed away a straying lock of her golden hair. Her blue eyes regarded father. She said, "Yes. I will urge her. And would you like me to come?"

"Yes," he said. And at the pressure of her hand, he added, "Oh, but don't you understand, Ahlma—Dianne seems to me just my little daughter—I love her."

"I understand." Her gaze still held his. In the blue depths of her eyes he saw a light twinkling like a smile. But her voice was very earnest as she added:

"And I will come also." The twinkling light in her eyes spread to a whimsical smile twitching at her lips. "What a handsome young man your son Drake is."

Half an hour must have passed. Or perhaps more. They sat, watching the small segment of floor into which we had vanished. There was a moment or two, father recalls, when it chanced that they were talking, and their glances strayed away. When they looked back, Ahlma gave a cry.

"I see—"

Father started to his feet, but she held him. He saw nothing. "What? What is it, Ahlma?"

"One of them!"

A single figure. A speck, there on the board. Ahlma lifted the lampshade. He saw it then. Something there—

"One of them!" she repeated. Her voice caught in her throat as terror swept her. "Only one! A man!"

She cautiously drew father forward. They knelt carefully on the floor, bending down over the board. A tiny figure there, an eighth of an inch long. But it grew. Half an inch! A man's figure. Clothes torn and blood-stained.

Drake! He lay on his side. But he moved. He drew himself up on one elbow.

An inch long now. He tried to stand, but swayed and fell back. He had spoken, but they did not hear it. He waved an arm.

A warning, but it was too late! Behind them as they knelt there was a footstep. They turned. Togaro—as large as Ahlma—leaped at them!

* * * *

Drake, down there in the caverns with the small figures of Dianne and me watching, fought with Togaro. He was aware of the shrinking walls. He heard and understood our tiny screams of warning. He scrambled up through the roof opening after Togaro. The space overhead was a caldron depression. They fought there. Togaro had been the first to take the drug. He was rapidly becoming larger than Drake. His strength was overpowering. They rolled together. Drake felt the big hands gripping his throat. He tried to tear them loose, but could not. It stopped his breath. He tried to heave his adversary off. But Togaro was too large. Too strong.

The lunge jammed them both against a wall which almost wedged them. It must have brought realization to Togaro. He suddenly cast Drake loose.

Drake's senses had almost faded; but with returning breath he strengthened. The walls were closing. Togaro scrambled out. Drake tried to stand up. His head and shoulders came above the closing caldron. He jumped; and as he scrambled out Togaro's fist caught him in the face.

He fell; and though he did not quite lose consciousness he lay motionless. Togaro struck him again. Beat him, kicked him. Drake had just the wits left to pretend insensibility.

This partly open space was again closing. A ravine in the corrugations of the upper surface. Togaro's attention was again distracted by the narrowing space. He evidently thought his adversary dead; or unconscious so that he would lie here and be crushed by his own growth. He left Drake. He leaped away, scrambled up and ran.

For a moment Drake lay quiet. He stayed as long as he dared. Then he tried to sit up. He had barely the strength to pull himself out as the ravine narrowed to a slit beneath him.

He fell prone. Togaro had disappeared. Drake lay amid the tumbled ridges of the upper surface. The ridges crawled and crept under him as his body grew. He was far enough out so that his body pushed itself over the surface undulations with its own growth. He fainted.

When he recovered consciousness—it must have been five minutes or so—he could distinguish the outlines of the giant room. He heard the rumble of father and Ahlma talking—their voices booming far up there in the radiance of the lamplight.

He was still growing. Togaro had escaped being seen by father and the girl. He had run to another corner of the room; stood quietly behind them, growing to their size.

Drake saw the monstrous forms of Father and Ahlma come forward. He lay on his side. They loomed over him—tremendous giants peering down with great faces far overhead. And behind them—almost equally gigantic—he suddenly saw Togaro!

Drake tried to call a warning. But they did not hear him. He was still weak and faint. He got up on one elbow. He gestured frantically. He saw the tremendous figure of Togaro leap at father.

Togaro's growth had stopped. He was as tall as father. His fist caught father and knocked him backward. He would have stamped upon Drake, but Ahlma saw the intention. She hurled herself at Togaro. Fighting, tearing at his face with her hands. And father assailed him also.

Drake saw the three huge figures swaying above him; Togaro, with a foot twice the length of Drake's body, was trying to get near enough to stamp upon him. Drake saw that father and the girl were being worsted. He tried to get to his feet, but he was too weak and dizzy. He sank back.

Then Ahlma broke away. She seized the lamp and flung it. The lamp fortunately was extinguished as it crashed to the floor. The room with its drawn shades, in spite of the daylight outside, was too dim for the small figure of Drake to be seen.

And then Ahlma began screaming. Togaro cursed. Perhaps he thought there was help near by. Whatever he thought, he flung father from him, and turning in the dimness, he fumbled for the door. Snatched it open; ran through the hall and dashed from the house.

CHAPTER 8

DEATH OF THE GIANTS

We returned to our normal size; and found Drake, father and Ahlma together. Father was shaken by his encounter with Togaro, but unharmed. Drake was bruised, battered and bleeding; but with his youth and strength he soon recovered.

The afternoon wore away. We had decided to start for the island as soon as it was dark. There was no sign of Togaro.

I talked that afternoon for more than an hour with Dianne. She told me many things of her strange world. Drake talked with Ahlma. I heard him say once, "You saved my life—he would have stamped upon me."

I recall with what a singular mixture of emotion I touched Dianne's hand. My adored little sister? A strange foreign princess? The two ideas, so wholly different, mingled in my heart. I recall, too, the flush on Drake's face, his low eager voice as he talked with Ahlma.

The darkness closed in around King's Cove. We were ready to start. Father, with an automatic in his hand, followed us down to the boathouse. We had tried to have him summon a car and go to the village earlier in the afternoon. Or summon help.

"Nonsense, lads—I can take care of myself. We've got to keep this secret. Why, suppose the authorities were to order that atom destroyed!"

The channel was black. The sea was calm, with a sullen, oily calmness. No giants had been reported. The lights of occasional patrol planes passed overhead; out at sea the lights of the waiting battleship were plainly visible.

Drake and I rowed swiftly, with the two girls huddled in the stern. I was tense, my mind roving upon a thousand weird unnatural dangers which at any moment might come upon us. But there seemed nothing.

The island loomed black and silent ahead of us. What was there?

I shipped my oar. We grounded on the beach. No sign of anything.

We prowled through the dark trees, with automatics ready. Drake had a small flash light. We came upon the embers of Dianne's signal fire of the morning.

Tiny figures stirred in the grass under Drake's light.

"Careful, Drake."

Dianne bent down cautiously. A microscopic voice called up to her. She said to us:

"They have not seen Togaro."

She led us a few feet to one side of the embers. "Drake, give me your light."

There was a patch of soft loam here, with grass and ferns growing in it. A small rock projected up in the grass. No one would ever have noticed it. Drake and I knelt down carefully over it. Dianne held the light.

It was the top of what seemed a bowlder buried here. Only a few jagged inches showed. Rock, scarred and pitted; coppery-looking. Metallic.

Drake murmured, "Why, this is a meteorite buried here."

It seemed so. We dug with our fingers in the soil around the projection. The thing bulged out underground. A meteorite that might have weighed a ton. Metallic rock, scarred and pitted and fused by the heat of its falling through the atmosphere to earth. Centuries ago it might have fallen, a visitor from the realms of space. It had buried itself here; or been buried since by the drifting silt of the passing years.

Dianne had known nothing of its being a meteorite. She showed us now the top projection. Made us understand carefully the exact point within which her atom was contained. It was easy to remember. A tiny crater—a pit into which a pin-point might go.

"We descend into that," she said.

We studied the configurations of the projection. With my hunting knife I could break off the top fragment easily.

She added, "Guard it somewhere—with that little crater held upward as it is now."

Ahlma said abruptly, "There is a storm coming."

Rain was beginning to fall. The clouds overhead were black. Thunder rumbled in the distance. And then there was a lightning flash nearer at hand. It brightened all the island for an instant.

Ahlma cried, "Look there! Did you see him?"

The darkness was already again like a wall around us. But we had all seen a giant figure looming into the blackness. A giant, here on the island beach!

Another lightning flash. The storm burst over us, with a surge of wind and rain. Upon the circular island beach, stationed at intervals, giant figures had grown into the sky. Six of them so huge that by leaning forward they might have touched hands across the island.

Dianne whispered, "We must get smaller! They can trample the island."

We were surrounded by them, trapped here—but even in our normal size we were so small that they evidently had not yet seen us.

In the glare of lightning as we crouched, we saw one of the giants lift our dory in his hand, crush it like a bug, and fling it out to sea. Another stooped and fumbled with his fingers over the island underbrush. He plucked up trees, as one would pull up stalks of fern.

But the section where we crouched, hiding now in a near-by bush, was undisturbed. Why, we never knew. Perhaps because Togaro was near here. Or expected here.

Already the presence of the giants was discovered. A war plane circled overhead, swooping through the storm. Its bomb dropped with a hiss into the near-by water. Then a shot screamed past from the advancing battleship.

Dianne gave us just a taste of the drug to diminish our stature. The island expanded. We crouched in a great jungle of forest growth which had been the thicket. Pebbles strewn here grew to great bowlders. We found a cavelike recess and squeezed into it. Miles of jungle and strange, dark land spread around us. Up in the sky, where the lightning flashed and a great torrent of water was pouring down, the bombardment of the island began.

The world knows of that night's events, that soon after nightfall six giants appeared upon Bird's Nest Island off the coast of Maine. They were attacked by the patrol planes.

The giants seemed great stupid brutes. Confused, perhaps. They plucked at the island's trees. They waded out into the water and back. They reached into the sea and flung huge dripping bowlders at the attacking planes.

The hovering battleship advanced. Its shots screamed at the island. One of the giants went down. He floundered in the water, with the others clustering in frightened amazement about him. Then his great body lay still. It sank, but rose again and drifted out to sea.

The planes dropped bombs. One of the giants, wounded, bellowed with cries that were heard all down the coast. He waded frantically out toward the warship which was some three miles off. But the ocean was too deep for him. He swam back. A shot struck him. He crumpled.

An upflung bowlder hit one of the planes and brought it down. The planes flew higher after that.

The coast was lashed with the waves of the giants' threshing bodies. Another fell; his head and shoulders sprawled across half of Bird's Nest Island.

The brief unseasonable electrical storm swept past. In half an hour of the battle but one giant was left. He tried to escape. He reached the mainland, staggering south. He fell, ten miles down the coast.

We crouched in the silence and darkness which had again fallen upon the island.

Drake murmured: "It's over."

Dianne took us back to our normal size. Sea planes were landing in the water of the channel. Clusters of lights showed where boats were heading swiftly for the floating bodies of the fallen giants.

Launches were putting out from the battleships. Other boats coming out from the mainland. A destroyer dashed up and anchored in the channel. Planes circled overhead. Activity everywhere. A dozen boats were advancing upon the island.

We had regained normal size. We stood in a group in the darkness of the island glade.

"We must hurry," Dianne whispered. "Frank, you understand—you chip off the fragment of rock. Wait a few minutes—ten minutes—after we are gone. Then you can't harm us. Take the rock home, guard it. Oh, Frank, keep it secret—and we'll come back some time."

Why all these directions only to me? I might have realized then, but I did not.

Dianne kissed me; Ahlma pressed my hand. The girls were already dwindling. The little figures of their escort lurked at our feet. I turned to Drake.

"We'll wait ten minutes and—"

I gasped. He too was dwindling. He said hurriedly: "I'm going, Frank. You explain to father."

I stood stricken. I recall his last words of instructions: "Togaro may have gone into the atom; or he may be here in our world. Watch out for him, Frank! These few giants mean nothing. Stupid brutes he has sacrificed—a test only of what he plans."

"But Drake—stop!"

I stood frozen. I was suddenly horribly frightened. Confused. A step, and I might kill them. I called, but there was only silence. I had the flash light, but if I lighted it I might blind them.

I sat down by the dead fire. Five minutes. Ten minutes. I heard boats landing upon the beach, and the shouts of arriving men.

But they must not find me until I had done what I had to do! I stood up hastily. With the flash light I located the projecting top of the meteorite. My fingers were trembling as I opened my claspknife. I recall that I was mumbling to myself:

"Steady, Frank! Don't do it wrong."

I knelt. I chipped at the rock. My pounding heart nearly smothered me. The tramp of advancing men sounded near at hand.

I hacked desperately. The rock fragment came off—a chunk a few inches in diameter. I laid it carefully in my pocket. I snapped off my flash. I huddled, shaking, by the wet embers of the dead fire. My brother!

Men surrounded me.

"What the hell?"

"Who is he?"

I stammered: "Let me go."

A turmoil of rough questions. "Who are you? What are you doing here?"

"Ferrule. My name is Frank Ferrule. I live over there—King's Cove."

Other men from another boat came up.

"I've heard of the Ferrules. House across there at King's Cove."

"Yes. That's where I live. My father's there now. I was here—got trapped here when the fighting started."

Somebody said: "He's scared stiff."

"Let go of me," I insisted. "Take me home."

They shoved me into one of their boats.

In the babble of excited voices I was soon ignored. I sat with my hand in my pocket, gently holding the precious chunk of rock.

CHAPTER 9

TINY FRAGMENT OF ROCK

A year passed. Father and I lived permanently now at King's Cove. In a special room, with three trusted guards, the fragment of rock lay carefully watched. Nothing—no one, friend or enemy—appeared during that year; and we began to think that perhaps no one ever would.

Father's health was not good. The shock of losing Drake was very great. He said it was not that. He said always—and so wistfully—that Drake would come back to us. And Dianne.

The world, for months, talked of those days of the giants. But the world soon forgets. The giants were an enigma—a menace—but our war planes and the battleship soon overcame it. No one, after a year, seemed afraid of giants; in a few years more they would be history, forgotten completely.

No drugs were found on the bodies of the giants. They wore, the reports said, a belt with many empty compartments. To whom could that possibly be significant, save father and me?

I sat often alone at night in the barred room, by the light which shone on the rock fragment as it rested on its smooth slab of stone. A microscope stood in a bracket which in an instant could be swung into position. Nothing could appear there without our seeing it at once. If the menace came, we were ready always to deal with it.

Tiny fragment of rock lying there, with its billions of atoms—each a universe. One—the universe that held Dianne.

I wondered, so often, what she and Drake and Ahlma might be doing down there in the Infinitely Small. Trying, perhaps, to protect us from the menace? It seemed so.

Often I cursed my helplessness. I could put my finger down and touch the fragment of rock. An eighth of an inch of space—no more than that, perhaps—separated me from Dianne. Yet it was an infinite, hopeless void of distance.

And then one night in May, as I sat alone, staring at the rock fragment, hope which I had thought dead leaped within me.

Something had come from the atom! Under the glare of light, where all these hopeless days and nights nothing living had ever appeared—something moved.

A speck, appearing from invisible smallness.

It grew.

A tiny human figure, small as a pinhead, was upon the jagged piece of rock. I swung the microscope over it.

And I saw a man in tattered, blood-stained garments, clinging to the rock, waving a white flag frantically at me!

CHAPTER 10

THE WHITE FLAG

Father and I had of necessity changed our whole mode of life when we undertook the watching of the rock fragment. We gave up our Westchester residence, to live the year around at King's Cove. Father moved his laboratory from Westchester; I relinquished my flying job.

The house at King's Cove, unheated, was not suitable for winter conditions. We installed a heating plant. We cleared out one of the small bedrooms. Barred its windows and its door, so that it had all the aspect of a cell.

The windows we sealed, not to be opened. A new door was hung, closely fitting so that there was not the smallest crack. Into the ceiling we cut a small ventilator to keep the air of the room fresh.

There was one small chair. In the center of the room there was a flat, six-foot-square slab of granite. It was raised above the floor on a sturdy pedestal. In its center lay the precious chunk of rock, with a dome-light over it—the white electric glare shining strongly down.

The microscope hung in a bracket; and there was another bracket—a rack of bottles and atomizers. Gruesome to contemplate using them! Bottles of acids and poisons; atomizers to spray poison liquids! These tiny humans which might appear would be treated like deadly insects, at once to be exterminated.

We had three guards employed. Between them, they covered the entire twenty-four hours. They sat armed with automatics. At ten-minute intervals they searched the fragment of rock with the microscope. An electric bell-switch was close at hand, so that in an instant father and I could be summoned.

Yet for all this neither father nor I could for a moment relax. Alternating with our hopeless moods that Drake and Dianne were gone forever was the feeling that Togaro might at any moment attack us. Within the atom thousands perhaps of his followers were preparing to conquer the earth.

It was nerve-racking business. Father was breaking down under the heart-rending strain of it. I knew he could not possibly go on for another year, living under such conditions.

There was never a moment when he and I both dared leave the house at once.

He was asleep this momentous night in mid-May. I had sent the guard out for a ten-minute relaxation. I saw the figure appear. I stood shaking, peering down into the small microscope. The magnified chunk of rock showed jagged and broken. Upon the upper lip of the crater-like hole the tiny figure was visible. A man, blood-stained and battered, with a waving white flag in his hand.

I turned from the microscope. I could just make him out with the naked eye—a pin-point of white movement.

I rang the bell for father. I stood trembling. Confused by the shock of this actuality which for so long we had been contemplating. A whirl of confused thoughts plunged at me. Was it Drake?

No! It did not seem to look like Drake.

A friend? An enemy? Should I kill it? What was I waiting for?

I became aware that I had seized an atomizer. A puff of it and a torrent of deadly spray would kill that tiny figure; and kill, doubtless, any others which might be there, too small yet for me to see.

I held my hand. A friend? A white flag—of truce?

The figure was expanding. Without the microscope now I could see it clearly in the brilliant white light.

Dare I let it get larger? I shouted: "Wait! You—stop!"

Father burst into the room. "Frank!"

And behind him the burly figure of the returning guard. Both were panting from running and from excitement.

"Frank?"

"Something here! Father, look! Man—with a white flag. See? See him wave it?"

Father seized the microscope. He was trembling so that at first he could hardly hold it. I clutched the poison spray; the guard stood behind us, alert with an automatic, and his gaze roved the room.

Father murmured: "Not Drake? Is it not Drake?"

"No."

"Oh—No, no, you're right—it is not Drake." The disappointment in his voice! "Not Drake—a man, a stranger."

I pulled at father. "You can see him now without the microscope."

The guard—a fellow named Foley, as near without nerves as a man could be—stammered:

"You—you going to kill it—him?"

"Yes! No! No, Frank!" Father clutched at me. "Look, he's climbing down."

The figure of the man was a quarter of an inch high now. He started climbing down the two or three inch jagged side of the chunk of rock. He slipped, slid; and then fell and landed upon the polished surface of the granite slab. He lay motionless.

"He killed himself, Frank!"

"No—look, he's up again!"

He was standing by the rock which towered like a cliff beside him. He was in a moment half an inch high. The white flag was a piece of white fabric. He had thrust it in his belt; he drew it out again and waved it wildly at us.

I said: "He's afraid we'll kill him." I put the spray back on the overhead shelf. "Think he can hear us, father? Understand us?"

"Yes. Maybe. Try it, Frank. Don't let him get too large. Tell him to stop. You see anybody else?"

Foley said: "I'll take a look." He applied his eye to the microscope.

"Don't shout, Frank. Slow, distinct. He'll hear you better that way."

I said: "Don't—get—much—larger! We'll kill you."

"Suppose he doesn't speak our language," father began.

Foley said: "Nobody else. He—this one—he's all smashed up. Bloody. You can see his feet; he's got 'em bound with rags."

The figure seemed to understand me. I could see the tiny face looking up. He seemed to be shouting at me. I turned to Foley.

"Wait, Foley. Quiet."

In the silence, as I bent down, the small words came clear:

"Don't—kill me! Friend—friend—from Drake."

From Drake! The word thrilled us. We stood breathless, watching the figure on the granite slab. An inch high now. A young man. Bruised and bleeding as though from arduous, desperate traveling.

His brief suit of knitted fabric was torn, dirty and blood-stained. His head was bare, showing his close-cut blond hair. His feet were wrapped into shapeless bundles with cloth seemingly torn from his garments. He stood wavering. He put the white flag into a belt at his waist—a belt which we could see now held many compartments.

Two inches high. He walked away from the chunk of rock. The light overhead appeared to dazzle him; he flung an arm before his face. But it seemed also that in the far distance he had seen the void which was the edge of the granite slab. He shrank back; then he looked up.

"Don't hurt me!"

His accent reminded me of Ahlma. Or Togaro! The thought came to me: was this a trap? This fellow with his white flag, was he from Togaro, masquerading here as a friend of Drake's?

Then triumph swept me. Here was the drug! This fellow had it!

Father was plucking at me as I bent intent over the growing figure.

"Frank, do we dare let him get large?"

The man was three or four inches high now. I put my face down close to him. It startled him so that he jumped backward and fell. But he picked himself up at once.

I said: "Can you hear me clearly?"

"Yes. Are you—is it you that are Frank Ferrule?"

"Yes," I said. "You stop getting larger. Stop, you understand? Then we'll talk. Are you alone?"

"Yes." He fumbled at his belt; then his hand went to his mouth. In a moment his size was unchanging. "Alone." He added, his tiny voice sounding clearly:

"Yes, here all alone. They wait for me in there—a portion of the trip in there, they are waiting with the flying car."

Father was whispering to me triumphantly:

"He's got the drug! With that, Frank, we can do anything. But we've got to let him grow to our size. Don't you understand—let him grow large and expand the drug with him!"

I had not thought of that. If this fellow were an enemy and it ended by our having to kill him, the drug he carried would be of no use to us. I stared down at his tiny figure, no longer than my finger. To a comparative giant like myself, of what use his infinitesimal quantity of the drug! We would have to let him grow large.

"What's your name?" I asked him.

"I am called Alt. I am sent to you from Drake. Trust me—do not kill me. I have a message for you."

Father said, "If you are from Drake—did he write to us? Send something to prove who you are?"

"No. That I mean—yes, he gave me a paper, but I have lost it. The journey was hard—"

Suspicion rose in me. But friend or enemy, we wanted his drug. I flashed father and Foley a warning glance. It would not be dangerous to let this fellow reach our own size—provided we were alert to keep him from getting any larger than us. I said:

"You're hurt. We'll dress your wounds. You can get larger—but be sure to stop when you are the size of me, or we will kill you."

He was docile enough. He said, "Very well, then I will do that."

He sat down on the rock slab and we watched him with a tense silence. In a moment he was a foot long; then twice that. His growing body pushed against the rock fragment. "Move!" I said sharply, "stand up—I'll lift you to the floor."

I ran my fingers over him; he seemed unarmed. I lifted him and set him on the floor at our feet. Foley moved the light to shine upon him; and stood with weapon ready.

Father cautioned grimly, "You obey us—no trickery."

He stood quietly eying us. High as my waist; then my shoulder. I said, "Enough! That's large enough."

I whispered to Foley; and when the figure ceased enlarging Foley pounced upon him.

"Give me that belt! The drug—give it up, damn you!"

He made no move to resist us. He stood meek—a slim young man now about my own height; and about my own age. He was pale and tired, in miserable plight, covered with cuts and bruises.

I seized his belt, stripped it from him. An affair of metal and fabric, with compartments in which were metal vials of the drug. Possession of it brought me a wild sense of power. Helpless no longer!

Foley backed the fellow to a corner of the room. "Stand there till they say what to do with you."

We were not afraid of him now. "Easy, Foley—don't hurt him!" I added, "Now you can tell us what you came for."

He said with a rush, "You do not trust me, but I speak truth. Drake—he is your brother?—he, with the Princess Dianne and the Lady Ahlma are in the flying car. Waiting. And they sent me out alone to you. I had a paper from Drake—I have lost it—"

"Why didn't Drake come?" I demanded.

"He stays to protect the princess. The men of Togaro are everywhere—in every size."

He almost convinced me, with the swift, apprehensive look he flung about the room.

Father said, "What was Drake's message? Don't you know?"

"Yes, I know. He wants—weapons. Our world in there is threatened—disaster—destruction of all our little world. Our people—following Togaro—have gone mad. Too gigantic for our little world to hold them! And yes, they threaten your earth too—but that you control safely out here in this room. Drake would have me tell you the invasion is coming. You must be watchful to kill them as they come out—and Drake wants weapons, to threaten them so that they may not go completely mad and wreck our little world."

Weapons? My suspicions leaped anew. Did this fellow think he could come here and we would give him weapons?

Father demanded, "What sort of weapons?"

"Not many—just two or three, for Drake to use to convince our people of his power. A knife-blade of steel—to bring death swift and silent. And he said, what you call automatics—two or three of them."

"Give you those and let you go in?" I retorted sarcastically.

His pale blue eyes opened wide. "Drake said you—his brother Frank, he said—would come with me. He wants you—I am to guide you to where he waits."

My heart leaped. Guide me in! Why, of course! From the moment I knew I had the drug, there had been in the back of my mind the knowledge that I was going in to Drake. I had not thought of a guide. Necessary, of course, if I were to locate where Drake was waiting. And here was the guide.

Father stammered, "No! I can't—can't let you do that, Frank. This fellow—a lying impostor perhaps, to lure you in there."

Would I go? Dare I risk it? I heard myself saying calmly, grimly:

"All right. I'll go in with you."

CHAPTER 11

GIANT IN AMBUSH

Within an hour I was ready. An hour of hurried, feverish preparation. Yet after all, there was not much to do. I wore a bathing suit, with a belt of the drugs strapped about my waist. And the stoutest shoes I owned.

Foley's eyes were never for a moment off this fellow Alt. He appeared inoffensive enough. He was not badly injured. Exhausted—he seemed only to desire a rest; he lay quiet while we bathed and dressed his wounds. They were bruises and superficial cuts where he had fallen on the sharp rocks of his outward journey. His feet were the worst. He had started with a pair of buskins, made of animal skin. The rocks had torn them to shreds; his feet were bleeding and swollen.

"Couldn't Drake get you shoes?" I demanded. "Something to protect your feet better than that?"

He smiled. A friendly, ingenuous sort of smile. I was alternating between liking him and being suspicious of him.

"No," he said. "We do not have what you call shoes. Drake did not know the journey would be so bad for me. It should not—I was not clever—I did it wrong."

"What do you mean by that? You got lost?"

"No. Not lost—I will show you what I mean, when we start in."

He had brought no food or water, and needed both badly. He drank the water we supplied him, and ate the bread avidly. The meat he discarded; he did not know what it was. He shuddered when we told him—as though to eat it would be cannibalistic.

I rigged a holster around my chest over one shoulder; and another about my waist, above the drug belt, so that I could carry four automatics and two or three knives. And with a cartridge belt, I was awkwardly equipped; I felt like a walking arsenal.

"I can carry some of them," Alt offered.

"No, thank you," I retorted.

He smiled, but made no further comment.

The trip in to Drake, he said, should only take a few hours. We would find water partway in; we needed little food. Alt suggested one small bit of bread.

A very casual fellow this! Certainly he hardly believed in preparedness. Suppose we got lost!

Strange journey! A trip, not of distance, but only of changing size. There were so many factors to it that I had yet to learn! Alt said quietly:

"Coming out, I used up my food at once. But going in that is not necessary." He saw my puzzled expression, and added. "If we put that piece of bread on a rock beside us, then in a moment there is a mountain of bread that could feed a thousand."

We were ready at last. Alt needed rest. But he seemed anxious to start at once.

"Drake bade me hurry."

We had bound his feet; and I found a large pair of shoes for him to wear over the bandages.

"Can you walk?"

"Yes."

"Try it."

He hobbled along the side of the room, with Foley eying him. His feet must have been painful; but in a moment he was walking with hardly a limp.

A likable fellow, this. He said, "I can do it. Besides, I shall be more clever going in—you will see. Our trip will be easy."

I said good-bye to father.

"Remember, dad, keep watch here. Closer than ever. And when we come back—look for our signal."

A flag of striped black and white which we would wave.

Alt explained the drugs. I would not let him touch them. The belt had eight compartments on each side. Two drugs, of opposite action. Eight intensities of each. Small, metallic vials held the tiny pellets.

"Have we enough?" I demanded.

"Oh yes, I think so. Or if we had not, it would be easy to set some aside, and pick them up again when we were smaller."

We stood in the center of the room on the floor beside the granite slab. Father sat in a chair. Foley stood regarding us as though we were ghosts and expecting us to dissolve into nothingness.

I handed Alt a pellet. "This right?"

"Yes."

It was the diminishing drug of the weakest intensity, like the one Dianne had given us, when in the bedroom we had pursued Togaro that brief distance into smallness.

"Yes," Alt repeated. "We each take one at the same instant." He touched me. "There is the great danger that we may become separated from each other. You understand? Lost in size. You will take none that you do not give me the same?"

"No," I agreed. Friend or enemy, I could not blame him for being apprehensive. I had the drugs; he had none. Lost in size—stranded.

We took the pellets. The familiar lurching sensation came as before. But this time I was prepared for it. I stood quiet, with the swimming room around me. I was facing the granite slab. It was waist high, with the rock fragment in its center. The slab seemed lifting; expanding—and receding. I was presently below it, looking up at its bottom resting upon the wooden supports.

Alt was unchanged beside me. He said in a moment:

"Your father will lift us up?"

"Yes."

My thoughts went winging off. I was not frightened this time. My heart was beating normally. A sense of eager exhilaration was on me. Soon we would reach Drake and Dianne.

I was abruptly aware of Alt plucking at me.

"Your father, he must lift us up!"

The slab was far overhead. At a distance, the wooden pedestal legs rose like great round columns of some strange, crudely-fashioned temple. I recall that just at that instant, I had the impression of a tug at my shoelace. A tiny twitch. But it was driven from my mind. I had no time to look down. Something gigantic came swooping at me from overhead. Something monstrous, pink-white, wrapped itself around me.

I was lifted. Squeezed breathless; and snatched up with a dizzy swoop. Up—a hundred feet it seemed, through the rushing air. Into a glare of light. And then released.

I saw the great pink-white hairy thing leaving me. It was father's hand. I staggered dizzily and fell upon a rough expanse of stone.

There are things which one sometimes can remember as being vague, unimportant impressions. Later, in the light of after events, they assume importance and one may wonder how they were overlooked at the time. The tug at my shoelace was such a one. And now, as I fell dizzily upon the stone slab, there came another. The feeling of something crawling upon me. As though an insect brushed my bare shoulder. I thought nothing of it at the time, but later I was to recall it clearly.

I heard a booming voice; father's voice.

"Oh Frank—have I hurt you?"

He had not. But I saw his gigantic hand and arm coming up more slowly with Alt.

I got to my feet, and looked up. Father's chest and head towered above me.

I shouted, "No, you did not hurt me. We're all right."

Again Alt plucked at me. "He waited too long! Hurry—run!"

We were on a naked expanse of uneven gray rock. It was flooded with yellow-white light. I saw, a few hundred feet away, a jagged mound of rock, large as a house. It was expanding, and drawing away from us.

Alt was running, and I ran after him. The expanding ground swayed beneath me. Alt called back:

"We've got to climb it—and it is getting so large—"

And so far away! I thought that we could not get there over the shifting, expanding ground. But we made it. The rock was a jagged, volcanic-looking mound when we reached it. Fifty feet high, at least. I followed Alt as he climbed up its precipitous slope. I was close under him; and suddenly I felt that if he were tricking me he had a perfect opportunity to turn and fling me backward.

"Wait a moment, Alt—let me get past you."

He stopped, and I led him to the summit. It was a long climb. We stood at last upon a rocky peak—in a yellow sunlight glare. Far down—it seemed five hundred feet now, at least—a great gray plain spread off into the distance. I could see a void off there—the edge of the granite slab. And vague towering shadows of form—father and Foley perhaps.

The rocks about us were still expanding with their crawling movement. A summit here, of tumbled naked crags. Fairly near at hand I saw a black hole—a pit. Alt led me to it. It was, by the time we got there, an orifice a hundred feet across. A pit of dense blackness, with perfectly smooth, almost vertical sides.

"We descend into that," said Alt.

My mind flung back. Dianne had used those same words, that night on Bird's Nest Island. This then, was the pin-point hole at the top of the rock fragment.

I stood with Alt, waiting. I was winded from the run, and the climb. My belts—the drugs—and the weapons—were awkward carrying.

Alt said, "If we had started just a little sooner, that climb would have been easy. We were too small. You see what I mean, using judgment in the trip?"

I did indeed. We were waiting now for this pit to expand further. The sides were too steep, too smooth now for descent. But the pit was widening; the walls were every moment becoming rougher. We had been quite near, but the expanding ground moved us away. I walked over to the lip again.

"The idea is to get down as soon as we can," I said.

"Yes," he agreed. "Shall we try it now?"

It seemed that there were places rough enough now to climb down. I had seen the bottom; it had not been very deep, though dark with shadow. But it was several hundred feet down now.

We picked our way, sliding perilously at times. We came at last to the bottom—a level, rocky floor, strewn with bowlders. The place seemed now a great circular valley, with towering mountainous sides. A haze of blue distance was overhead for a sky. A pseudo-sunlight was up there; but here on the valley floor shadows made an unnatural twilight. I noticed too, a different quality of air. It was dryer, with a vague metallic sharpness.

"Which way?" I demanded.

The drug we had taken had reached the limit of its effect while we were descending to the valley pit. The landscape was no longer changing.

A new world already. A barren desolation of rock. I added:

"Do we take more of the drug now?"

Alt stood a moment considering. "There is another descent which I think we can almost make in a leap. This way—it is not far."

We walked along the valley floor. The heights from which we had come were beside us. A wildly tumbled volcanic region. There were narrow rifts, cracks in the bowlder-strewn floor; pits, and tiny craters, some with upstanding rims, as though lava had welled up and congealed. Corrugations; ridges; little buttes, and peaks like spires of needle-point sharpness.

I got the sudden impression that I was very large, and that this was a landscape all in miniature.

I was walking beside Alt. "How do you know where we should go?"

"Not far from here there is a place like a crescent. It should be—for our size now—quite small and not very deep. You understand? Easier for us to jump down into it now, than to make a long climb when we are smaller."

We rounded the corner of a fallen mass of bowlders, as though here an avalanche had come tumbling down the valley wall.

"Over there," said Alt. I saw, down a short slope, a small, crescent-shaped pit, with a span of a few feet. We were some two or three hundred yards from it.

I was suddenly stricken motionless. I stood gasping, with the shock of surprise and fear. From the pit, the head and shoulders of a man rose up. A giant face, malevolently staring. His body filled the pit. His hands appeared, caught at the rim, and he scrambled out.

And, with a shout, Alt turned and ran at me!

CHAPTER 12

THE MEETING

For that instant, I was convinced that I was trapped, lured here by Alt to this giant lying in ambush. But Alt shouted:

"Run—that is a Togaro man!"

As Alt went past me, I saw his fear-stricken face. The giant—three or four times my own height—was climbing to his feet. Alt was heading for the broken cliff wall. I ran after him.

Behind us the giant came with a bound. The cliff was fifty feet away. Alt shouted back a warning—something about hiding in a small cave-mouth. There were many small openings; we must get into one too small for the giant to follow.

There was no time for us to take the drug. No time to do anything but run. But in a moment I knew we could never make it. I could hear the thud of the giant's running footsteps, rattling the loose rocks. In a moment more he would have us.

I shouted: "I can't get there, Alt!"

Alt stopped abruptly. He bent and seized a chunk of rock. Futile stand! A hundred feet away the giant came leaping. He was larger now.

Then I thought of my automatics. In the shock of this sudden encounter I had completely forgotten I was armed. I whipped one out, and stood like a hunter facing a charging elephant. But mine was the trembling courage of desperation.

The fast-growing giant was forty or fifty feet tall now. My automatic felt like a toy as I leveled it. I fired; blindly perhaps at the last. The giant let out a bellow of rage and pain—and astonishment. He leaped sidewise; he stood fumbling, clutching at his shoulder where my little bullet had stung him.

Alt shoved me. "This way—run!"

We reached the cliff bottom and found a narrow cleft running back in the rock wall. It was only a few feet wide, but we wedged into it and forced our way back a yard or two.

The giant was silent now. In a moment he was outside the crevice, but he was far too large to get in. We heard him poking about; mumbling to himself. Then he seemed to be digging, rattling the rocks. His hand and arm came into the passage probing for us, and I fired again. The report was deafening in this confined space. Powder fumes choked us.

The giant let out another roar, and his arm, wounded no doubt, was withdrawn. He vanished. In the silence, we heard the scuffle of his heavy, retreating footsteps.

We were all but choked; yet we did not dare go out. We crouched, gasping, and presently the air cleared. There was silence. "Shall we chance it, Alt? Or get smaller in here?"

"Try outside," he whispered. "I think he is gone—getting large, on his way up."

We crept from the rift. The valley outside seemed empty. The giant had vanished. Or was he around here somewhere?

I whispered: "We'd better not move—it might attract his attention."

"No. Wait for a time."

We crouched in the deep shadow of a bowlder. No question of Alt's loyalty now, and my instinctive liking for him sprang anew.

"That was a close call, Alt."

"Yes."

I added, "You want one of these guns?"

In the gloom I could see his pleased expression. I showed him how to aim and fire the automatic. He wore a belt to which was strapped a package of sandwiches and a vacuum of water; I threaded the holster on it.

We waited, perhaps five or ten minutes, crouching by the rock with the silent, shadowy valley around us. There was still no sign of the giant. There were cañons here, into any one of which he might have plunged. The silence was heavy, oppressive, eerie. A haunted silence, as though here were things not to be seen or heard, yet nevertheless making their presence felt.

I whispered at last, "Shall we start?"

"Yes."

I had been lying on my side, raised on one elbow. There came a movement at my belt; I sensed a tiny indefinable creeping movement upon me. My hand went down with a swift, instinctive gesture—as one moves with a startled hand to knock off an insect. And Alt gave a low, sharp cry.

We both saw it at once. As I sat erect, a small human figure which had been clinging to my belt at the side, scuttled down my leg and leaped off me to the ground. It vanished in the shadows. We made a hurried, startled search, but it was gone. We had briefly seen it—a man the length of my thumbnail.

"Gone, Alt!"

We searched no further. Impossible task to find such a figure here on these dark rocks.

The thing gave us a shock. We crouched again, waiting, silently listening. This strangely fearsome journey! Nothing alive save ourselves, here in this brooding place of rocks. Nothing to see, or to hear. Yet it seemed as though there might be living multitudes around us. Humans, not moving in space very far, yet journeying. The giant was gone. He had passed us, moving on into largeness. This tiny figure which had been clinging to me was rushing ahead of us perhaps into smallness.

Alt's voice checked my reverie.

"I think it is safe to go on."

We started off again. The crescent pit we found to be some twenty feet deep. There was no trouble descending its broken sides.

Alt said: "Coming out, I could have climbed in this size very easily. But I was smaller. I climbed up here—it seemed a thousand feet."

The giant had evidently been in here, growing, and had waited until the last moment to scramble out. He had been as surprised as ourselves, no doubt, at the sudden encounter.

"There must be many of Togaro's men traveling," said Alt. "They are in every size, traveling, exploring."

This darkling abyss of rocks! I conjured enemies lurking in every shadow ready to spring upon us. Giants—or tiny humans smaller than insects. Enemies of every size and of shifting stature.

We kept steadily upon our way. The crescent pit opened into a valley with towering mountain ranges for its walls. Then we entered a tunnel mouth. Timing it with unaltering size between one of the pellets, I saw it as a miniature tunnel which our bodies almost blocked. We followed it, from one gloomy cavern to another—a distance seemingly only a few paces. Yet I could envisage that with another pellet it would be a black march of hours in a vast dark void and a desolation of rocks. An army of our enemies might be marching here like that now!

We encountered no other Togarites, yet I think that many were passing close to us in size. Going out, I wondered? If they showed themselves, father and Foley would make an end to them promptly.

We stopped once and ate our sandwiches, keeping one of them only against disaster. We finished the water in the vacuum bottle. There was water now occasionally to be seen in pools on the rocks.

The landscape had been continually changing. The light from overhead was long since gone. Occasionally we were in some tunnel or cave of darkness. Yet there always seemed a little light—as though the rocks themselves were radiating a glow.

The air was changing. A brittle crispness. A dryness. And then, when at the termination of the effect of our fourth pellet we found ourselves on a vast metallic plain sloping down into darkness, it incongruously began to rain. A slow, fine drizzle. Overhead I could see moving dark clouds.

We came upon a patch of soil, almost barren, but not quite, for there was sickly vegetation struggling in it. Tiny green things growing. Clumps of them, with small rock ridges a foot high lying like snakes.

The drizzle was fine as a mist. After a few moments, it ceased. Abruptly I realized that the puffs of cloud were very small and close over our heads. And again my whole viewpoint shifted. I was a tremendous giant standing here, towering to the clouds. A tiny forest was here at my feet; the ridges were rocky ranges of hills.

I strove to encompass thought of the journey as a whole. We had been only a few hours. It seemed that we had descended thousands of feet into the bowels of some vast world of naked rock. Perhaps we had. In our present size, I am sure the entire trip would have been miles of distance. Yet to father, up there now in that inconceivable titanic world, we were still near the surface of the porous rock fragment.

We took another pellet, and the landscape grew.

Alt gripped me. "See—the light!"

A steady red spot of light was visible near by.

Alt said: "Drake's signal."

We saw Drake first. He stood in the growing forest as our dwindling bodies came down into it. The red light painted his figure as he leaned against a stunted tree-trunk.

"Frank!"

"Drake—Drake, we see you!"

We adjusted our size. He came running forward. He called back: "Dianne! Ahlma, Dianne—they've come!"

It was so good to feel his handclasp!

"Father all right, Frank?"

"Yes."

"You've got the rock guarded?"

"Yes, Drake, we—"

And then I saw Dianne. The glory of her beauty swept me. She ran up and kissed me.

"Frank, dear—"

I do not know what I was to her then. But to me, this was not my sister. A thousand times more strongly now, I felt it. And no princess this. Just a girl!

CHAPTER 13

THE STOWAWAY

We stood in the shadows of the dark forest, with its gnarled, stunted trees. The red light flamed near by. A dim figure glided up to Drake. He gave an order; the figure hastened away. In a moment, the red light vanished.

Drake spoke hurriedly. He and Dianne and Ahlma were leading Alt and me toward where the red light had been. Drake half whispered:

"We saw you coming—lighted the red signal for Alt. Dangerous to keep it lighted now; Togaro's flyer has been here. His men—they may be near this size—would capture our flyer if they could."

We hardly went a hundred yards. To my questions Drake was impatient. "Presently, Frank. Here, this way."

I saw, in an open space, the dim shape of an interplanetary vehicle. An elongated globe, forty feet long, with its bulging middle half as wide. It lay dark and silent; but I saw that it had elliptical windows and a small doorway which stood open to receive us.

Strange vehicle! As we approached I could see that what I had thought was a dead-black thing of metal was in reality far different. Drake hurried us up a small ladder, into its interior. But I saw that the vehicle's side was not solid.

It seemed rather a myriad woven wires. The thing was a big cage, woven of intricate metal threads like a basket. Rigid, yet resilient.

I learned afterward some of the details of this strange vehicle. Standing inert, as it was now, the outer air circulated freely through it. The wire, of which its hull and all its interior ribs and braces were composed, was drawn from a ductile metal unknown to our world, a metal which contracted or expanded freely under the impulse of an alternation of electronic current. With the current charging it, the hull became a solid electrical surface, with the entire interior an active magnetic field, so that ourselves and all the contents of the vehicle were contracted in size as the hull diminished.

No drugs were needed now. We could use them inside the vehicle merely to change our size in comparison to the vehicle itself.

There were chemical air-renewers, and heaters to keep the interior warm against the cold of interplanetary space.

An interplanetary voyage! I could not at first grasp it. No vast space was here. We were in a dark forest, with a limited mountain valley around us. No stars were overhead; no great astronomical reaches were here. Where could this vehicle go? Into smallness, I knew that. But how? Sail off over these stunted trees? Why, in a moment with any speed at all it could reach the mountain barrier down which Alt and I had just come.

But I knew, as I pondered, that if this flyer remained just where it was, as it diminished in size, sufficient space for any flight would open up around it.

The door was barred behind us. We passed along a low, narrow passage, walking on a metal grid of woven wires. I saw small rooms; ladders leading up and down to other levels. A small room, crowded with strange instruments faintly throbbing as though all this wired bundle of mechanism was impatient to be gone.

We came to a little room with a window in the concave side of the hull; a table of woven wire; and a few wire chairs.

"Sit down," said Drake. "You particularly, Frank—be careful as we start. Your first voyage! The shock is different from the drug. I see you brought the weapons?"

"Yes. Do you want them now, Drake?"

"Keep them. We'll look them over presently. Sit quiet, Frank." He spoke hurriedly, abstractedly. "We must get started at once."

He hastened from the room to give orders for the starting. I had seen some eight or ten men aboard the vehicle. Four were in the instrument control room; Drake went in there.

I sat down, with Dianne beside me. Alt was whispering to Ahlma near by. Dianne murmured:

"Don't talk now—just for a moment."

I sat waiting. This vehicle with its many small rooms; its small passages, gave me again the impression that I was too large for my surroundings. Drake had stooped as he went through the arcade into the adjacent control room.

The dark trees showed motionless outside the window.

Dianne murmured: "Now, Frank."

It was a slow transition. The wire walls of the room turned faintly luminous. They hummed. A dull red glow suffused everything. The wire floor, the ceiling, the chair upon which I was sitting, all glowed red, like wire slowly heating. Red, then yellow, then almost white, with a cast of violet. But my hand on the chair-arm felt it to be cool as before.

I was conscious of a slight shock. A lurch. But it was within my head, for the room did not move. Everything was glowing white. Yet the room remained dim, for the light did not radiate. There was a throbbing; a hissing, whining sound of the surging current.

Then the air of the room turned electrical. It faintly snapped; occasionally in mid-air, a burst of small blue sparks exploded like a bomb. The outlines of the walls and ceiling and the furniture were lit with tiny blue lightnings.

Then I felt the real shock. A swoop of all my senses; a second, in which I thought I was gone, falling, with only the consciousness of Dianne's firm hand holding me.

A moment, then the shock was passed. I steadied, and found that save for an unusual lightness and a tingling, I felt no different from before.

Dianne murmured: "That's all, Frank; you're past it."

"Yes. Have we started?"

"Oh, yes."

Drake came back. He eyed me appraisingly, but made no comment. He sat beside us.

"Let's see what weapons you brought. Frank, did you encounter any of Togaro's people? His flyer brought some out. A few. Not many yet. We haven't seen Togaro—we don't know where he is. But his expedition is ready. They don't know that we control the fragment of rock—that they cannot escape from it. They're coming out."

"If they do, father will stop them."

Drake was willing enough to talk now. He said: "Yes, father will stop them. That doesn't worry us. But in the atom—in Dianne's world—did Alt tell you? They've got a single vehicle, like this one, Frank. They keep it hidden. We can't find it—or haven't been able to, yet. Togaro's leaders are winning our people, firing them with desire to conquer the earth."

Dianne said: "When we get there—but, oh, Frank, I'm so glad you've come!" Her hand lay on mine; her fingers had gone cold. This was no regal princess—just an apprehensive, frightened little girl. Glad I had come! The weapons I had brought might be of use in this affair. But myself—what good could I be, trying to cope with a nation in revolt? Yet instinctively she turned to me.

"I'm worried, Frank. These are my people—this is my world at stake. The Togarites are telling our workers that never will they have to work again."

Drake interrupted passionately: "Dianne has told them they can't conquer the earth, that we control things up above! But they don't believe it. So now I'm going to threaten them. A bullet—they'll think that's magic. A knife thrust—and, Frank, we can't use the size-change as a weapon in Dianne's world. We dare not grow too large. You'll understand—you can understand now if you think of it. The Togarites' leaders have the drugs. They lurk everywhere in a size abnormally small. Sometimes they grow gigantic. But they dare not get too large.

"You see, we cannot fight them in largeness upon Dianne's little earth. There is a limit to what is safe. We have avoided such combat, and so have they. But they are more daring now.

"Their main expedition into largeness is about ready. It's all being done secretly—Dianne and her government are powerless to stop it. We think that a multitude of her people are willing to join Togaro's expedition. The leaders have been waiting for Togaro, but he has not come."

I said, "Because he's out in our earth-world and can't get in."

"Yes, doubtless. And now they won't wait any longer. The disaster, in spite of everything Dianne and I have been able to do, is now upon us."

My mind groped with these strange things he was saying. A group of a hundred or more Togarite leaders had for years been in possession of the drugs. They had built themselves an interplanetary size-changing vehicle, like this one in which we were now traveling. They kept it hidden—in some small size, doubtless. Dianne's controlling government would have destroyed it, but they could not find it.

The drugs were kept from the public, of course. But these bandit Togarite leaders had them; and they could not be discovered and confiscated either.

The Togarites wanted, Drake said, about a half million followers. With this multitude they would conquer the earth and populate it with their own race.

"Why?" I demanded. "Why do that?"

My question sounded inane. Drake shrugged. "Why has any conqueror lusted for power? The original Togarite leaders are evil fellows, renegades. Togaro himself tried to conquer Dianne's world, and failed. They want power, riches, plunder. Togaro wants all that. And he wants—Dianne."

I could feel Dianne stir against me. I said nothing, and in a moment Drake went on:

"There are ten million of Dianne's people, upon a little globe which they populate fully. Just the one nation. Perhaps by now the Togarites have their half million followers. They plan to transport them out—up to our world—"

"How?" I demanded. "A single flyer, like this, to transport five hundred thousand people! Why, it would take thousands of trips! Ten or twenty years—"

But as I said it, I understood why that was not so—and comprehended the deadly danger to Dianne's world. I began: "If they make their vehicle large enough to contain half a million people at once—"

I never finished.

Once before, in the room at King's Cove, Ahlma had given a cry to warn us of impending danger. She did that now. She and Alt were sitting near us, listening to our words. Drake had previously taken the automatics from me. We had put them on a vacant chair; one lay on the floor close by my feet.

I heard Ahlma give a startled cry. The automatic on the floor had been lying between Drake and me. I remembered clearly where I had placed it, but it was not there now! I followed Ahlma's glance. The weapon was on the floor, over by the wall. It was moving—sliding soundlessly toward the door of the room. I saw that a small human figure was tugging at it—a man eight or ten inches high As tall as he dared get. The weapon was larger than himself. He was struggling to drag it to the doorway, get it beyond our sight.

Ahlma's cry made us all leap to our feet. And Dianne and Ahlma together recognized the tiny figure.

"Togaro!"

He dropped his burden and scuttled from the room. Dianne gripped me. "Wait, Frank! You're unsteady yet—you'll hurt yourself."

I found the floor swaying under me as I stood up; I had to drop back.

Drake and Alt dashed into the passage. We could hear their cries giving the alarm. Several members of the crew came running. The passages and all the cabins were searched.

Useless! Togaro had taken the diminishing drug. With such a start, he had escaped into smallness beyond pursuit.

Drake and Alt came back. "It was too dark. We could not see where he went at all. No use trying to follow him."

Togaro, a stowaway on board!

CHAPTER 14

THE LOCKED DOOR

Amazing voyage into smallness! I find an adequate picture of it difficult to paint. It was, as Drake had said, a voyage shorter in time than I had been led to expect. Fifteen or twenty hours of elapsed time, perhaps. We tried to preserve a normality of routine. We ate several meals, and I tried to sleep. For the remainder of the time we sat in that small room, by the window; and I gazed at a panorama so singularly awe-inspiring that I am at a loss now to describe it.

For some time the ship did not seem to move. We sat talking. There was obviously no movement. The room was steady, save for a humming vibration. But outside the window things were changing. The forest trees were sliding upward. Expanding, and drawing away. We were dwindling faster than an intensity of the drug. Then I felt the ship lift slightly. We hung poised in a rocky void.

I conjured all manner of wild, gruesome thoughts. Nor were they all picturing danger to myself or to Dianne's world. Nor even the threatened conquest of earth. There was a danger that seemed to me now greater than any of these. Togaro desired Dianne!

I sat close by Dianne. I tried to tell myself that there was nothing to fear. Togaro would not dare get large, here on our ship. For if he did, at once we would seize him.

We discussed it. The thing seemed incredible, that he was here so close to us and we could not find him. Incredible, but true.

We stood at the window, Dianne, Drake, and I. But Alt and Ahlma would not relax their watching of the room. The ship had been dwindling now for more than an hour. The forest was gone.

I saw a dark void, in which seemingly we were hanging in mid-air. At first I thought it was wholly dark. But as I stared, with my eyes—or perhaps merely my mind—becoming accustomed to this pregnant darkness, I found that there were things to see.

We hung motionless in the void. But presently rock walls were visible; how far away I could not guess. Great mountains of rock, expanding, sliding upward, and drawing away, though they did not vanish. It seemed that my vision must be sharpening, or that the light was increasing. It was a strange sort of light—an iridescence, vaguely diffused throughout everything.

For a long while this went on. The visual sensation was that we were falling like a swiftly dropping elevator car. But it was not so. The rock walls were sliding upward, but it was largely an optical illusion.

A meal was served us. The ship was reaching a greater intensity of its shrinking size, dwindling more rapidly.

I could hear the current rising to a higher, sharper and louder whine.

Drake said, "That's a hundred times faster for us now."

Another few hours. The scene outside was undergoing a progressive change. The distant rocks constantly had a different aspect. I could not fathom it—could not define it. A suggestion of roundness. I stared at the far-away wall. It seemed as though great round things were piled in loose masses. A wall of bowlders loosely piled.

Once, I fancied that they were in movement—creeping, crawling, one upon the other. And that all the wall was unsolid. A thing of slow, ponderous movement.

I became suddenly aware that once more my viewpoint had abruptly changed. I had envisaged us as a tiny ship, hanging in a great dark void, with dark round things at some inconceivable distance. And then I saw it was not so. We were a tremendous ship! These round objects were tiny particles. Close at hand. Dark, yet glowing. Moving, sliding one upon the other with a suggestion of fluidity. Nor were they just here in this one direction. With my face against the window I could see them overhead. And below. And across the near-by corridor of the ship, a window there showed them the same on that side.

From everywhere they crowded us. Abruptly it seemed that we were not in a void, but in a narrow, confined area with these particles jostling us. They were all of a size—all of a similar aspect. Tiny things, with space between them. Flowing like a fluid as we pushed our way among them.

Drake said, "They are molecules, Frank. The molecules of the rock fragment. We'll soon enter one—and then enter our atom."

I did not answer him. My thoughts went winging off. Millions of molecules here. Millions? Countless myriads. They shifted and crawled; jostled; swept past, and away. Then there seemed a darkness as of an empty void. But always I saw them again.

The scene was always changing. Open space now, with banks like clouds of the clustering molecules in the distance. I fixed my attention upon one such cloud. It was coming rapidly nearer—or perhaps we were speeding toward it. A luminous cloud. It came up and went past. The molecules were huge and few. I thought perhaps in that group there were not more than thirty.

Clouds speeding, with dark voids between. Why, this was space! Gigantic space here.

Then I saw just two of the round things jostle past. And then some which went by all alone. Giant things now, glowing, unsolid! I began to think I could see that still other, smaller particles were clinging together to form each of these unsolid molecules.

I saw one go past, and caught a glimpse of what seemed empty space within its luminous outline—and then I could almost fancy I saw the atoms, a whirling swarm of them clustering to make this unsolid outline.

Drake's words rang in my thoughts. Enter one of these molecules? Find our atom?

I said, "Drake, how can this ship be guided? How in Heaven's name can we—"

He told me—or tried to tell me. I am no scientist, to put down here abstruse explanations of a subject so vastly unknown. Nor would I obtrude them into this narrative. I recall that Drake explained how by a shifting of gravitational force this vehicle could be guided for space-flight. That I understood. The bow of the ship made attractive—to receive the gravitational attraction of whatever masses of matter lay in that direction. And the stern made repellent, or neutral, at will. All that I could understand. An interplanetary flyer, of the sort which often on earth had been contemplated.

The size-change principle was also comprehensible in fundamental generalities. But how, upon this inward trip, could we search these myriad molecules for one particular molecule? And then find one atom? And within that atom find one electron—or a proton, whichever it might be—within which was a vast reach of astronomical space?

Drake called our guiding instrument a spectrometer—an instrument tuned to the vibrations of Dianne's world. He spoke of being able to search out the characteristic spectrum; he spoke of electronic resistance factors; of the aura of this designated world we sought, its atomic force which, as we approached it—or receding, went astray—was shown upon our instrument, thus to guide us.

Let the textbooks explain it. There are many such now being published. I can record only those things I saw and did. And they, in truth, are strange enough so that I can only affirm my veracity and let it pass at that.

Beyond our windows came a void of emptiness, with only occasional single molecules drifting past. They were always larger. Then I saw them as objects enormous. Great dark worlds of that unsolid stuff we call solidity!

Drake insisted that I try and get some sleep. The ship was being patrolled end to end for any sign of Togaro; but there was none.

Dianne urged, "You must sleep, Frank. We must all keep normal. There will be so much to do when we arrive."

"Tomorrow," said Drake.

Tomorrow! So incongruous a term! All normality of time or space seemed gone. But I did try to sleep, and for a while must have done so, for I dreamed a phantasmagoria of shifting things in a void of blackness.

I wakened to find Drake alone at the window.

"The girls are sleeping, Frank. No sign of Togaro. Sit here by me."

He had an automatic in his hand. We both wore belts of the drugs—and a belt with holsters for the other weapons.

"Look, Frank."

We had been in the vehicle now some twelve or fifteen hours. I was astonished when Drake told me I had slept four hours at least. I saw outside the window now a scene wholly different from before. We had reached, and been maintaining now for a considerable time, our fastest rate of diminishing size-change. Much faster than near the beginning of the voyage, and conceivably faster than the most rapid rate that the drugs could give.

I gazed in awe from the window. This was astronomical space indeed! I saw a vast reach of blackness, with blazing stars. Great suns, resplendent with a corona of flame. White, dull red—some of them yellow. They lay strewn like gems on a black velvet cloth. Some were in clusters, faint as luminous dust in the distance. Above us there was a great band of glittering star-mist, like the Milky Way.

The whole brilliant scene was swift with electronic movement as of stars. But I realized that our vehicle was not only dwindling, but sweeping forward in a flight of tremendous speed. The stars went by in a steady drift. The heavens in advance of us seemed opening up; the points of light sped past our window and drew together behind us.

Tremendous celestial panorama! I was lost in awe watching it. There were spaces of blackness devoid of stars. Sometimes, far off to the side, a lens-shaped cluster would drift past, to be lost in the distance behind us. A universe of itself. Or a great spiral nebula—I saw one which with a visible movement seemed rotating.

Then ahead of us another universe would come. A faintly luminous patch. Spreading wide as we sped toward it—until all in a moment, it seemed, after crossing an empty void we were again among stars. Great suns blazing alone. Or binaries, rotating with slow dignity about a common center of gravity. Or suns, with smaller, dark worlds swinging in orbits around them. Planets! We could see some of them, shining like moons in every phase; and some held satellites of their own.

We had for hours been within the atom. And one of these planets, somewhere here ahead of us, was Dianne's world!

I gazed, and there grew upon me presently the realization of a very strange aspect to this glittering scene. These blazing worlds were not large!

It caught at my breath, this realization. I regarded a flaming point off to the side. It was drifting backward. A monstrous world of incandescent gas, millions of miles off there? I suddenly realized that was not so. Why, it was a mere pin-point! An enduring spark! It was not far away, but close outside our window. A monstrous, giant sun—yes. But our vehicle was still so infinitely larger! Why, this was no vast reach of space—not compared to us!

I saw us plunge into a myriad points of light. A universe of stars. But they were still so small in comparison with us, that we crowded our huge bulk in among them. I saw some of them strike against our hull—pin-points of fire harmlessly tiny.

We went through an incandescent cloud of them; they bombarded us like a rain of sparks. We plunged through and came again to a cavern of emptiness, and then another universe, appearing ahead of us.

I could see now the effect of our dwindling. These sparks were growing, expanding steadily.

Drake had several times left me to consult the men in the control room. He said once, as he returned: "You see, Frank, what I mean by haste. We are chancing it." His tone carried an apprehension. "There are millions of light-years of distance to be covered in here. That is, they would be light-years when we were small. While we are large they can be crossed in a brief time. If we were to wait until we were smaller, and then make the voyage, this space-flight would take weeks, months perhaps. Yet we dare not cause too much astronomical disturbance. We must be normally small before we approach Dianne's world—not to disturb it in its orbit."

I said, "Are we near there, Drake?"

"Yes, near in time. They've just told me our forward flight must stop. From here, a size-change only. And then, when we are safely small, a short voyage—and then we'll land."

"How long, Drake?"

"They said a few hours."

He sat down beside me. The scene outside the window had another, more familiar aspect now. The side-drift of the stars was stopped. They were widening out. Shifting both upward and downward, and receding from us as we grew small among them. I fixed my gaze on one which was level with our window. It seemed moving away. Drawing away to a great distance, yet it always remained visually as bright as before. A tiny spark, growing to a great blazing world.

How long a time passed as I sat there, absorbed, I do not know. Two hours or more, undoubtedly. Drake occasionally talked, and I answered him vaguely. They were still diligently searching for Togaro, but it was a fruitless quest.

I recall that I suggested we might use care in disembarking, so that Togaro would be kept a prisoner in smallness here on board.

But that was impractical, as Drake at once pointed out. Togaro could easily make himself an inch high and still be reasonably safe from our observation. No use for us to guard the vehicle doorway. When our size-changing current was cut off, the wire hull of the ship was not solid. A figure an inch high could squeeze out through the side of the hull very easily. Of what use to guard the door!

"We can't get him, Frank. If he's cautious, handles his size right, he's safe from us."

Safe from us! But the thought, like an omen, swept me: were we safe from him?

I said, "Shouldn't the girls wake up by now?"

It seemed that they had been sleeping a very long time; Drake and I had had another meal served us.

"They went in just before you woke up, Frank. Only three hours—the rest will do them good—they were worn out."

He had already told me that they were being carefully guarded. But now, as though it were a premonition, a fear grew upon me.

"Can't we go see them, Drake? Make sure they are all right?"

He gave me a startled glance. "Come on."

I was steady enough on my feet now. We went into the small, dim passageway. It was whining and throbbing with the electrical sounds of our size-change. An uproar of rhythmical throbs—one could shout along here and scarce be heard above it.

As I got to the door, my heart pounded. Their guard was in his place, fifteen feet down the shadowed passage. But there was something unnatural in his hunched position as he sat with his back against the wall. His head seemed to have sunk forward upon his chest. Asleep?

His hand on the floor held the automatic. His head was slumped. I shook him. His inert body twisted, and fell sidewise. And we saw, sticking in his chest, a tiny sword like a bodkin plunged skillfully between his ribs to reach his heart.

Murdered!

The door to the girls' staterooms was closed! We jerked at it. Locked on the inside. We pounded, shouted, kicked at it frantically.

There was only silence from within.

CHAPTER 15

TOGARO AT BAY

The silence was horrible. If the girls were in there, why didn't they answer? We thumped and pounded.

"Dianne! Dianne, answer us! Ahlma—Ahlma—"

Our cries brought members of the crew. The body of the murdered guard was shoved aside. We jammed the passage, assailing the stout metal door which was glowing with the current in it.

"Dianne—Dianne dear!"

The door resisted our efforts. We stood listening; I put my ear against the door.

Only silence. It seemed that even a scream would be less horrible.

"Break it down," exclaimed Drake. "We must hurry!" He flung his powerful body against it, but the door held. Alt came running with a metal bar. We rammed. The passage was too narrow to give us room. But at last the door yielded a little and we got the bar into the crack and pried.

We burst into the room. Ahlma lay upon the bed, unconscious. Her robe was torn; there were bruises upon her temple, her shoulder and arm. The room showed evidences of struggle.

Dianne was gone!

Ahlma had fainted or been knocked unconscious. We revived her presently. Meanwhile we were searching the room, examining every inch of it for tiny human forms who might be lurking in the shadows, still large enough to be visible.

But there was nothing.

"Watch the doorsill!" Drake commanded. "If he's here—he may make a rush to get out—"

They carried away the body of the murdered guard; two men knelt, with faces close to the doorsill, watching it.

But there was nothing.

We knew, even before Ahlma revived, what must have happened. Togaro, with an inch or two of height, armed with a needle-like sword, had crept upon our guard in the passage. Amazing, reckless villain!

He must have dared to crawl upon the guard; then leaped, plunging his little sword like a long needle into the guard's heart.

Then he had scuttled into the girls' room, to grow large and softly close its door. He had fifteen minutes, probably, before we discovered the murder.

Ahlma revived and told us the rest of it. She had been awakened to find Togaro—in a size nearly as large as herself—forcing a pellet of the drug upon Dianne. The girls struggled and fought. Their screams, barred by the closed door and the humming, throbbing ship, had not been heard. Togaro had taken the diminishing drug, and forced some of it upon Dianne. He had struck at Ahlma. Her senses faded. Her last memory was the sight of Togaro standing in the middle of the floor with Dianne gripped in his arms. Both he and Dianne were dwindling.

We searched the room again. But we could find nothing.

Were Togaro and Dianne still here? If he was still here, we could keep him here in smallness. If he had got small in the center of the room it might be hours, or days of marching to reach the doorway and through it to the passage, even if he could find his way.

Drake cried, "By heaven, we won't land! I'll keep this ship in space until we find him! Starve him out—there'll be no food probably, here in smallness on the floor of this room."

But starve Dianne also! I was shuddering. Dianne here—down here by my feet perhaps—here with Togaro, hiding or wandering in some desolate abyss of smallness. Or perhaps we had already trodden upon them!

We stood with sudden terror, hardly daring to move. But were they here? I said, "Let's try getting small, Drake. We've got to try something. Get small here—in the center of the room where Ahlma says she saw them. Search for them. Drake, we've got to get her away from him!"

I was talking wildly and I knew it. Drake gripped me.

"Wait, let's try and figure it out. Easy, Frank—don't let's lose our wits."

It seemed as though every moment was vital. I stood listening to Drake's theory. Theory, at such a time! A surge of self-condemnation was upon me. If only I had had the sense to stay close by Dianne!

Drake was trying to estimate what Togaro had done. This door had been barred on the inside. But there was a crack under the bottom of the door an eighth of an inch high, at least. Drake closed the door for a moment and showed me it.

"Frank, they could be anywhere. Not here in the room—he wouldn't stay here in the room—he had fifteen minutes maybe."

With sinking heart I realized how easily he could have escaped out of here. He and Dianne, diminishing say to an inch. Then walking to the locked door. Dwindling again—walking, carrying Dianne—through the crack under the door.

He had had fifteen minutes—and another fifteen had now passed. He could indeed be almost anywhere in the ship.

There was a sound near by—a scream! Not that exactly. A shout. It sounded above the throbbing, humming of the ship.

We stood frozen, listening.

"Drake, you heard it? Where was it?"

He murmured, "What was it? A voice—"

Not in this cabin. We stood listening in the doorway. Diagonally along the passage on the other side was the door to another small cabin. It stood open. Had the shout come from there? We had searched all the cabins ten minutes before. We did not dare move without extreme care. An incautious step might crush Dianne.

There was a guard out here in the passage. All the crew were forbidden to move except with the greatest circumspection. The guard said, "It sounded in there. Shall I go?"

A moment of waiting. I murmured, "Drake, over there."

It came again, unmistakably from that opposite cabin. A single shouted word, but we heard it.

"Frank!"

Dianne's voice!

We rushed. No need for caution now. Hardly more than a dozen steps to that open cabin doorway. But as we reached it, the heavy door clanged violently in our faces!

We stood baffled. We shouted. "Dianne! Dianne, are you in there?"

From behind the barred door came Togaro's jeering, sardonic laughter.

"We are here. Come in and get us—if you dare!"

CHAPTER 16

FRANK'S PLAN

This door, like the other, resisted our efforts, to smash it. Alt ran to get the bar.

We called, "Dianne!"

She did not answer. With my ear against the door, it seemed that I could hear a movement inside.

"Dianne! If you can speak, answer me!"

I thought I could hear a low, gruff murmur. I demanded, "Togaro! Open the door!"

No answer.

Drake shouted, "Damn it, we'll break it down! Here, give me that bar!"

We assaulted the door. In the silence between our blows, Togaro's mocking laugh sounded again. It chilled me; horrible, sardonic, confident laughter.

The door began yielding. I warned, "Drake, your automatic."

He handed the bar to Alt and the two men of the ship's crew who had joined us. Ahlma, white and trembling, but eager, stood among us. Drake swept her behind him. He and I stood with weapons ready.

"Now, Alt."

With a last blow the door fell inward. From where we crowded in the passage the front portion of the little cabin was exposed. The huge legs of Togaro were bent like a jackknife as he sat wedged in the room! We could see at first only the lower half of him.

Drake jumped into the doorway; his weapon went up. Togaro's voice sounded—a dull gruff roar.

"Wait, you fool! Do not kill me!"

It checked, for that instant, the shot that Drake might have fired. I was beside Drake now. The whole interior of the cabin was filled with the huge body of Togaro. He sat sidewise to the door. The knees of his bent legs were nearly as high as our heads. His back was jammed against the stateroom bunk; his head as he sat hunched forward, crowded the ceiling. His body was wedged solid into the little room.

And upon his lap, held against his chest, Dianne was standing upright. Her head came hardly to his bent shoulders. His arm encircled her.

The scene froze us for an instant. The giant, evil face of Togaro, above Dianne's head, leered down at us.

He said, "Do not kill me! Do not dare! Dianne, tell them to talk to me—not to shoot."

I met Dianne's gaze. Her size in relation to me, was about normal. Her face was pale, but she seemed unhurt. She gasped.

"Frank—Drake—don't try to kill him—you don't understand—"

Why not kill him? He was holding Dianne in front of him—but from where I stood I could have sent a bullet into his brain and not endangered Dianne.

Or would his death throes have crushed her? I did not dare fire, yet. Drake felt the same. He lowered his weapon; he pushed mine down.

"Wait a minute, Frank. Easy."

Togaro's smile widened. His broad, heavy face had a look of monstrous evil. He said, "Why, that is better. Now we will talk."

"What do you want to say?" Drake demanded. "Let Dianne go. Dianne, climb down—"

It brought a gibe. "How can she climb down?"

I said, "We've got you. I can put a bullet into your head in a second. Do you know what a bullet is?"

"I know. Yes, young man, I know very well. But you won't do that. Quiet, Dianne—stand quiet, I am not hurting you."

His tone changed wholly as he admonished her. Ironic, to me; gentle, solicitous, and yet ironic also, to her.

I threatened, "But I will! We'll give you one minute!"

Drake pushed me back. "What have you got to say, Togaro? You're caught. You can't get smaller—we can kill you in an instant with these deadly weapons. You can't hurt us."

He was indeed so wedged into the cabin that he could scarcely move. But Drake was making empty threats. Togaro interrupted him calmly, "Can't hurt you! But you cannot kill me so fast that I will not also kill Dianne. Crush her to death; here in my arms. Quiet, sweet one, I am not crushing you—yet."

We saw now that Togaro's hand held a pellet of the drug, a pellet expanded to the size of a marble. He showed it to us.

"The enlarging drug. I think I can get it into my mouth, Drake, before you can kill me. It will be effective ten minutes at least after my death. Did you know that? Ten minutes of my body growing, here in this small room—"

He left the sentence to our imagination. Across his huge lap the cabin window was visible. Outside it I could glimpse the black void of space—a dull-red crescent hung out there, with white stars blazing around it.

Our ship was here in space. A growth of Togaro's body, and he would burst the roof of this cabin and wreck the ship.

Drake stammered, "But you—you would not dare—"

"Nor would you," Togaro returned calmly. "You do not want me to crush Dianne. Or break this tiny ship and kill us all. I do not want it. Fear nothing, I am no more anxious to die than you. There is of it nothing for you to fear. I would not like to hurt my little Dianne." His hand encompassed the span of her shoulder and back with a gesture like a caress.

We knew we were defeated. Drake said, "Yes. What do you want?"

"Go now and tell them in the control room to land as soon as possible. That is simple."

Drake turned away. "You watch here, Frank. Keep him covered."

I stood, a few moments later, in the passage whispering with Drake. We had an hour of grace. Togaro, from the window beside him, could see our progress toward landing. We did not dare do anything else with the ship.

But there was an hour. And I had a plan. Desperate; to me, with my inexperience in these strange conditions, it was a plan incredibly awesome. Yet I could think of nothing else which might be done. A plan by which I might rescue Dianne and kill Togaro.

I whispered it to Drake.

He said at last, "Yes, I guess it's the only thing. You think I should go with you? Two of us—"

"No. The chances are better with one."

"Then I will try it," he said. But I shook my head.

We stood out of Togaro's sight and hearing. Ahlma was with us.

Ahlma said, "But, Frank, you are not used to it. If you would trust it to a girl—"

But that was not feasible. Drake would have been better than I, no doubt.

"If I do not come back," I urged, "you, Drake, are needed here. And when the ship lands—it is you who are needed, not I."

It seemed the best thing to do. I had an hour before the landing. And I was ready now. I needed no preparations. I wore my belt of the drugs; I carried a knife like a short sword.

I edged up as close to the doorway of Togaro's cabin as I could get without his seeing me.

I took the diminishing drug.

CHAPTER 17

THE TINY PROWLER

"Good-by, Frank," Drake reached carefully down and touched my dwindling shoulder with the tip of his finger. "Be cautious—don't take too many chances."

"No."

"Remember—if he once sees you—well, that's the end, Frank."

I called softly upward. "I'll be careful. You give me the signal, Drake, when you think I'm small enough to start toward him. And remember the plan. If I can distract his attention—if Dianne leaps away—you shoot him."

I was already not much higher than Drake's shoe top. The passage floor was in shadow. The wall was drawing away from me.

I had taken what was perhaps half of one of the pellets of the weakest intensity. Its effect was gone in a minute or two. I stood quiet, trying to judge my height compared to Drake; and waiting for his signal to tell me that I was small enough to dare advance into Togaro's doorway.

A scene of singular strangeness, here on the floor of the shadowed passageway! The floor was a grid, or grill of laced metal. I saw it now as a spread of level surface; girders three feet wide, with others crossing to checker it into squares—three-foot squares, each of them a black abyss. The perpendicular passage wall was fifty feet from me. The other way, I could see Drake's monstrous figure; it blurred up into the distance overhead. I gazed, trying to estimate his apparent height. Four hundred feet tall, or more. Beyond him— it seemed a quarter of a mile at least—there was the blur of Ahlma's robe.

I concluded that to Drake I was about an inch high. I saw him move; as though some great dark mountain were falling upon me, his body stooped above me. His hand came slowly down; his palm spread like a pink-white roof close over my head. And then swooped upward; I could feel the suction-wind as it rose.

It was our agreed-upon signal. With my heart pounding I turned toward the cliff which was the passage wall. I walked, half ran upon one of the broad metal girders.

I came to the wall; followed one of the girders going lengthwise of the passage. This huge passage! A vaulted, shadowed place five hundred feet across, and twice as high.

Ahead of me the cliff ended in a great opening. Togaro's doorway! I stopped at the edge of it; stood cautiously peering. I could see into the gigantic room. Togaro's back seemed half turned to me. I could distinguish only his foot and leg. The blur of his body showed in the upper distance; and Dianne up there—a dim golden blur of her robe.

I took a few more steps. It was several hundred yards into the room to reach that huge foot.

But in my present size I could not cross the threshold without the chance of his seeing me. I had nearly an hour; I decided to get smaller.

A taste of the drug. The girder beneath my feet widened until it was a broad, rough metal roadway.

Space above me and to the sides was so great I seemed almost in the open. Ahead in the distance there were dim blurs of shape. And there seemed occasionally the muffled rumble of monstrous voices.

I ran until I was winded, then walked. How far, I have no idea. It seemed, altogether, a mile or more. The roadway ended in a great spread of rough metal surface. I climbed a gentle slope like a mound, passed over it and descended.

The threshold! I was in the room.

I had been advancing toward the mountainous outlines which were Togaro's body. I came near them now. He wore rough cloth trousers. The corrugations of them were tremendous fantastic ridges of gray surface rising into the air.

I stood again trying to fathom just where I was, and what I might do. I was still a considerable distance from where those billowing folds of cloth rested upon this metal ground. I ran again, then walked to get my wind. I was already tired. The gray mountain was at hand. I think I was behind Togaro. The folds of his trousers rose in an almost formless shape to where, several hundred feet up, I thought might be the line of his belt.

I stood beside his leg. I even touched him. The cloth was like woven strands of rope. Each strand was rough with dangling edges.

I put my hand upon one strand. It was as thick as the rope that ties an ocean steamship to its dock. There were spaces here into which my whole arm would go.

I set my foot into an opening. I could climb this! I gripped one of the strands. I swung myself up.

Then realization came to me. Why, this was madness! There was five hundred feet of height above me, and then I would only reach the ledge which was Togaro's belt. All this time his least movement would fling me off, plunge me to my death.

Madness! I let go, and leaped backward to the ground. I would have to get larger.

I took a cautious taste of the enlarging drug, then another.

The scene around me, with its steady dwindling, began to rationalize. I found myself standing behind Togaro, in the curve between him and the stateroom bunk. His waistline came down. I thought that presently with a leap I might reach up and seize his belt. Or in a moment I would be able to climb into the bunk. And from there perhaps leap upon his shoulder.

I had, for a long time past, been aware of various sounds. I had heard Drake's voice in the passage, talking, I thought, with Togaro.

The expanding drug action ceased. I drew my sword. I was now, I think, compared to Togaro, a foot possibly in height. There were sounds—a confusion of them—in the air. Voices, blurred by the mingled throb and hum of the ship.

But abruptly they all changed. A silence. The new sounds—a clanging, and a sudden voice! Drake's voice:

"Dianne! Togaro! Sit still or I'll kill you—"

I was stricken. Togaro's great body, with Dianne clutched to him, was heaving, rising.

He lurched backward, almost to crush me. Drake shouted again, but his words were lost in the turmoil. It seemed that all the world was crashing about me—rending, tearing crashes.

I leaped upward. My sword dropped as I clutched frantically to keep from falling. I caught at a great leather band, wedged my arm under it and clung.

I felt myself heaved monstrously into the air.

CHAPTER 18

THE ESCAPE OF TOGARO

It was an anxious time for Drake, this hour during which he was waiting for me to make my attack on Togaro. He stood, with Ahlma behind him, watching me dwindle. Then he stooped, cautiously keeping back where Togaro could not see him, and gave me the signal.

I was about an inch high, down by his shoe. His gaze followed me as I ran toward the doorway. In the shadows there he saw me getting still smaller, until I was lost to his sight.

Drake whispered to Ahlma, "We must act naturally." He put his arm around her in his apprehension for Dianne and me and the knowledge that there was disaster ahead for us all. "Ahlma."

She whispered, "Drake!"

They could find no words, but needed none. For a moment he held her, kissed her; saw in her misty eyes an answer to the tumult of his heart.

"We must be alert, Drake. Be ready for what may come." She turned abruptly and called into the ship, "Frank! Oh, Frank, you go to the control room and tell them again to hasten our landing. Drake and I will watch here." Calling so that Togaro would hear her and not be suspicious that I was not in evidence!

Drake whispered, "Good idea!"

Alt came up. He said aloud, "The ship is diminishing very fast. We will be there soon." He added, in a whisper, "He is gone?"

"Yes. Stay here with us."

The minutes dragged by. Togaro sat quiet; he held Dianne close to him; occasionally he spoke to her. Sometimes he would command Drake, "Remember, when we land—if you do not try to harm me, Dianne will be safe."

Through the windows Dianne's world was constantly visible. It lay now beneath the ship—a great spread of convex, red-brown surface. The light of its parent sun gleamed upon the mountain tops. The configurations of the land and water areas were plainly visible, save where, in patches, cloud masses obscured them.

The vehicle presently was dwindling quite slowly; then its size-change ceased. It dropped swiftly down toward the globe's surface.

There are a few brief astronomical details which I think I should record. When Drake and the ship landed now upon this little globe Drake was normal in size to its inhabitants. Calling him then his earthly standard of six feet tall, a comparative set of measurements may be given of this atomic world.

You who read this can visualize only by earthly standards. That is natural, for to the human mind the conception of one's self is the starting point of every comparison. During all these events I recall that I almost always felt myself to be my original, normal size. I saw landscapes which were huge, and landscapes small as children's toys.

But always I felt myself to be Frank Ferrule, five feet seven inches tall. Thus quaintly egotistical is the human viewpoint; to each man is his own mind the pivot of the universe.

Dianne's earth within the atom, then, you may visualize as a globe with a diameter of about three hundred miles. A circumference something over nine hundred miles. Its inhabitants were far larger, therefore, in comparison to their globe, than we are to our earth. To them it was indeed a little world—small as an asteroid would be to us.

It was called, in the native language, "Mita." A blazing sun was near it—twenty million miles away, perhaps—and Mita was the only planet. It rotated on its axis with a revolution of about six hours and forty minutes; so that, as we experienced the passage of time, the equal days and nights were each about three and a third hours in duration.

There was a slight inclination of its axis—a progression of seasons with a cycle of some three months. There was one small but brilliant moon.

Again, I can only say that textbooks are now being filled with the astronomical technicalities of the planet Mita. I record only such few stray facts as may make my narrative more understandable.

There was, for instance, the gravity as we felt it on Mita. In spite of the globe's smallness, its inhabitants felt a gravitational pull not much different than we feel it on earth. This was caused by the planet's tremendous density. A solid little globe of heavy, metallic rock.

* * * *

It was night when the vehicle dropped through Mita's atmosphere, heading for the largest city of the world's single nation. Drake stood in the passageway within sight of Togaro and Dianne. There was a window near him. Through it he could see the landscape as it rose and visibly expanded until presently it seemed close underneath the ship. The sunlight had faded from the sky when the ship entered Mita's shadow. It showed now as a line of red-yellow light on distant mountain tops. A fading light—the sunset, with the brief night just beginning. The sea was off there beyond the mountains; and again a line of ocean showed in the opposite direction.

Directly beneath the ship was an island-continent. A land-locked lake with many islands was near its center. A curving reach of lakeshore showed a patch of checkered, shadowed surface which was the city. Overhead a half moon was hanging.

Drake still had Ahlma and Alt beside him. They were watching Togaro— pretending to watch him, but in reality their anxious gazes were searching for me. I was, I think, at about this time lurking behind Togaro. I had reached a size where Drake could have seen me, of course, had he dared advance into the doorway and look; but he did not.

Increasing apprehension swept Drake. The time was growing short. He had ordered the ship to land. It was already filled with the preparatory sounds: the voices of the navigators in the control room giving orders, the rattle and clank of moving chains, the opening of a side door for disembarking.

Drake's apprehension grew into a panic. He had thought, of course, that I would make an attack before this. He did not dare now give orders to have the ship kept in the air. Togaro was watching through the window at his side—his glance darting out there and then back at Drake. The giant held Dianne's small form close against his chest.

He had admonished her not to speak. He kept her face turned now from the doorway, with his huge arm encircling her. And he forced her to reach up and with her tiny hands clutch at the collar of his shirt.

Through the window there was presently the close-at-hand moonlit vista of the lake, the shore front, and the city buildings. Drake saw the familiar landing-space. It came swiftly mounting, only a few hundred feet down now. A crowd of people, dark figures edged with silver moonlight, stood gazing up at the dropping ship.

Ahlma murmured, "What can we do?"

A sudden confusion gripped them. The ship was landing! To Drake it unreasonably seemed as though this sudden crisis had plunged upon him all unawares. He had waited too long for me.

Horror swept him now. Togaro's hand went to his mouth. He took the enlarging drug! A clanging resounded through the ship. It tilted, thumped slightly, came to rest upon the ground. For perhaps five seconds the three in the passageway stood transfixed with horror. Then Drake shouted:

"Dianne! Togaro, sit still, or I'll kill you!"

But it meant nothing, and Drake knew it. He gripped Ahlma and Alt, and flung them back against the passage wall, staring with futile, helpless horror.

The already huge body of Togaro was expanding. But already he filled the small cabin. He lunged, heaved his shoulders up against the ceiling.

Drake shouted again, with more rationality this time. "Togaro, don't hurt Dianne!"

Togaro panted, "No!"

He held her in the protecting hollow of his arm. He rose, straining his shoulders once again against the ceiling in a monstrous lunge. The ceiling broke.

Togaro stood a moment in the wreckage, expanding until only his giant legs remained in the cabin. Then he leaped upward. With a single jump he cleared the ship and landed upon the ground, scattering the terror-stricken crowd.

A growing giant, with huge bounds he fled away down a moonlit road toward the lake. The crowd on the landing field, staring after him, saw the small figure of Dianne hanging to his neck.

At the back of his waistline they saw a far smaller figure. It was I—clinging desperately to his belt, riding him like a clutching insect of whose presence he was unaware!

CHAPTER 19

NIGHT OF TURMOIL

Drake hurried with Ahlma and Alt from the ship. It was a scene of wild confusion as the frightened crowd milled over the moonlit field. In the distance the figure of the running Togaro loomed, a huge dark shape towering over the landscape. This little world was visibly convex: the horizon was very close. Drake could see Togaro bounding along the road which followed the lakeshore, beyond the city outskirts. His giant figure sank lower until presently it was gone below the horizon.

The crowd, which had been watching the giant, redoubled its confusion. Men and women were here; even a few children were held aloft to keep from being trampled. The near-by throng surged upon Drake.

Alt gasped, "They saw a man hanging to Togaro. Very small."

"Frank!"

"Move—back—" Alt began in English, then burst into a flood of his native language.

The crowd was pressing close upon them. Drake had all he could do to protect Ahlma from the roughly surging people. They were all about Alt's size—men bare-headed and barelegged, with jackets long to the knee, flaring like a skirt; women, some of them dressed like the men, but with hair bound on their heads, or young girls with longer skirts and flowing hair.

Drake, who wore the native costume, with a band about his forehead to hold his hair from his eyes, stood head and shoulders above the crowd. He held an arm about Ahlma, and struggled to force his way across the field. His instinct had been to take the enlarging drug and follow Togaro. But that was not practical. Togaro, always able to be the larger, could have turned upon him. And with Dianne in Togaro's arms—and now myself, so tiny, clinging to him—Drake realized that any combat would only kill us both.

"Ahlma, we must get over to the field-house."

"Yes, Drake."

"See the officials. There should be someone here to meet us."

The crowd had seen the ship descending and had gathered. The officials were here. Drake saw a line of the native police guarding the ship, and at the little field-house there were others.

Alt said, "There is Jain." He called to the official, a huge black-coated fellow. Drake knew him; and he spoke English.

Drake said to Ahlma, "Everyone's frightened. Give way there!"

But the crowd was more than frightened. Menacing, Drake abruptly realized, as two men roughly plucked at him.

"The drugs!" Ahlma gasped. "They want the drugs."

Jain came wading forward, bellowing with the voice of authority which now the crowd began to obey.

Drake called, "I don't want to hurt them." He was far stronger than any of these people, and he was armed, both with the drugs and the weapons I had brought. But this was a crowd of Dianne's people.

Drake had lived among them for a year; he knew them well, and they knew him. They were an excitable people; in a panic of terror now at the sight of the giant Togaro. Drake had no wish to do anything to excite them further.

He shouted with what he hoped would be reassuring words. Alt shouted in his own language. They forced their way forward.

The mob presently began dispersing. Jain led Drake into the field-house, a small building of metallic blocks. Other officials were here. There was a hurried consultation.

Then a conveyance arrived—a long, low wagon on rollers, with a covered top and a line of small animals to pull it. They climbed aboard and rumbled off through the city streets to the palace of Dianne.

I never saw, except with fleeting glimpses, this Shore City, as its name might be translated into English; nor Dianne's palace, nor any of her loyal people, the Mitans, as the nation was called.

To Drake it was all familiar. He had attained a position of authority. The ruling class—those who were born with the crescent patch on their foreheads—had accepted him as one of them. Dianne, headstrong little ruler, had insisted upon going in the flyer when Alt was sent out into largeness. Now, in spite of Drake's efforts to guard her, she had been taken by Togaro.

Jain was very solemn. "The council will blame you, Drake."

They could not blame Drake more than he blamed himself. Yet, from that moment Togaro held Dianne in his arms there was nothing Drake could have done.

And nothing now that he could think of to do. He sat immersed in gloomy thoughts. For all his year among these people it was still a strange world to him. He said suddenly: "Jain, that was my brother clinging to Togaro. We've got to find where they went."

Jain was solemn, but there was an excited triumph upon him. For months now the Togarites had kept hidden in smallness. Their headquarters—the place where they kept their interplanetary ship—could not be found. The Mitans had searched. Thousands of organized searchers were scattered everywhere throughout the land. For months no Togarite giant had ever appeared.

But now Togaro's arrival would disclose where his followers lurked.

"We will get the news at the palace, Drake. We'll know now—and we will organize an army, with the drugs and your weapons, and go after them, Drake. We will get them now!"

It was a ride of no more than ten minutes. The narrow city streets were lined with low houses, all built of metallic blocks. There were few lights, for the night was cloudless and the brilliant moon bathed everything with silver.

The city was in a turmoil. Crowds thronged the streets, milling and shoving and shouting.

The cart nosed its way along. The identity of its occupants was known. Drake often heard his name shouted. The crowd opened for the cart, but closed in behind, and followed it.

They wound up a hill, and entered the tree-shrouded gardens of the palace. It was a scene of almost normal earthly beauty, with paths and flowers, and low-stunted trees, heavy with redolent blossoms, all shining in the white moonlight, with a gentle warm nightbreeze from the lake.

The palace was a long building some forty feet in height, overgrown with climbing plants like some ancient castle of earth. Two stories, and an unusual dome roof like the crown of a helmet surmounted by a needle-spire. There was a single broad doorway up a short flight of stone steps. The lower windows at the ground level were barred. But overhead was a broad balcony with a metal railing, with open doors and windows giving access to the second floor rooms.

The palace faced the garden on this side, and on the other stood sheer upon the brink of a cliff—a perpendicular rocky wall, a hundred feet down, at the bottom of which the waters of the lake lapped on a narrow rocky beach.

As the cart rumbled across the garden, Drake caught a glimpse of the lake beyond the corner of the building. A moonlit spread of placid water, sharply convex. At the near horizon a green island loomed in the moonlight. The cart stopped, and they hurried into the palace.

The garden behind them was jammed with the arriving mob. A silent, gathering throng. Ominously silent.

CHAPTER 20

IN THE BLOOD LIGHT OF DAWN

Drake leaped to his feet. "But this must be stopped! Good God, this is madness!"

An hour or more had passed. The brief night was more than half over. Drake had sat in the palace with the harassed council. Night of turmoil! This brief night, preface to the end.

It seemed as though all the city sensed it. The crowds were in a wild chaos, surging everywhere throughout the city. Aimless, leaderless mobs.

The government, too, was in chaos, striving to do a multiplicity of abnormal things at once. A welter of official activities was around Drake. He sat watching and listening, waiting an opportunity to take his part in the one thing most vital to him—the expedition which soon was to start upon the rescue of the Princess Dianne, and the capture of the Togarites.

The whereabouts of the enemy was known now. The island at the nearby horizon held them. It was no more than three miles away across the water. A public garden and park occupied this small island. No one lived there, but pleasure parties often went to spend a few hours. The island had been searched many times and nothing found.

Yet it was Togaro's headquarters, quite evidently. His giant form had been seen wading out there. He was there now. Drake from the palace balcony had stood and seen the towering figure in the moonlight. And then it had dwindled. In smallness there, beyond doubt, the Togarite ship was hidden. He and his leaders were there.

Drake listened to the council making its plans. An expedition of young men who had been trained in the use of the drugs was now being assembled. They were coming into the palace now, in groups, as the messengers sought them out in the city and brought them.

There seemed only one way to get to the island unperceived by Togaro. The spaceship in which Drake had arrived was being hastily repaired. In an hour or two it would be ready. A hundred young men, and Drake with his automatics, would board it. The ship would then dwindle to a size very small. It would seem a flight of miles to the island—but the ship could do that in a brief time. And in such a small size could land unobserved.

The cause of the turmoil in the city was puzzling and disturbing to the council. The arrival of Togaro had created an excitement almost verging upon panic. But the excitement had started before Togaro's arrival. All during the three-hour daylight preceding, and the night before that, a strange air of unrest had been apparent among the people. There were fifty thousand of them here. The near-by rural districts held another fifty thousand. There was an influx from the country into the city. No one knew why. Whole families coming in their carts, then abandoning the carts, and mingling with the city crowds.

Messengers arriving from other cities reported the same conditions. The people everywhere were frightened, acting strangely. The small government flyer came on its four-hundred-mile voyage from the other side of the globe. It was mostly water in that hemisphere; but there was one island—one large city. It, too, was in a turmoil.

A strange restlessness, which the panic here in the Shore City over Togaro's arrival could not explain, pervaded Mita. To Drake it was as though by some occult force the knowledge was spreading throughout the world of impending doom. But he knew it was nothing occult. Might it not be that Togaro's followers were dispersed widely over this little globe, mingling with the people, spreading insidious, frightening propaganda?

The minutes passed while Drake sat watching the arriving men whom he was to lead. The council room was in the upper story. The men came up, were checked and given instructions, and then taken to the lower floor to be equipped with belts and the drugs.

Word came that the spaceship was not badly damaged. The repairs were progressing. It would be ready for the voyage by dawn.

All this time, in the garden of the palace the mob had stood unnaturally silent, watching the building as though trying to guess what activities were going on inside. Messengers were constantly arriving and departing. Police were bringing in the young men whom Drake was to take into smallness. The airship from the other hemisphere came and landed near by; its officials hurried in through the police cordon at the palace doorway.

As though nature were conspiring with a premonition of what the future might hold, a cloud lifted above the horizon across the city and passed near the moon; a cloud at a considerable altitude, tinged with red from the coming sunrise. It threw a red cast upon the moon. The moonlight suddenly seemed drenching all the scene with blood. An omen? Drake shuddered. He turned from the window. But the murmur down there grew to a shouting. It brought his gaze back. A rhythmic shouting—the repetition of a few words over and over. It may have started with a single voice, and the crowd took it up like a chant.

"Alt, what is that?"

Alt was near Drake. He listened. But Ahlma caught it first.

"They say, '*The world ends tonight! Give us the drugs!*'"

Like a chant the crowd was all shouting it now. "*The world ends tonight! We want the drugs!*"

The council heard it. A silence fell upon the room as they listened. Then from the palace doorway, the police began shouting. A new turmoil, then the sound of thuds upon the front palace walls—missiles were being thrown. A chunk of rock came hurtling through the window. It narrowly missed Drake and fell with a crash in the midst of the sitting councilmen.

It was then Drake leaped to his feet. "But this must be stopped! This is madness!"

The mob was attacking the palace doorway. It surged at the foot of the steps. A rain of rocks came hurtling upward.

Drake shouted, "Jain, tell the council I'm going to get large! I'll disperse this mob—Ahlma, you come with me! You can talk to them—try to calm them! Tell them you are speaking for your princess."

A turmoil almost equal to the confusion in the garden now broke out in the council room. The men were all on their feet, jabbering excitedly.

Jain shouted, "No! They say no, Drake—"

Drake was spurred by the feeling of helplessness that had made him stand by and watch Togaro escape with Dianne.

He handed Ahlma a pellet. Alt pleaded, "Let me come with you."

Before the council could move to stop them, all three had taken the drug. The room began dwindling. It struck a sudden calmness to Drake. He said:

"Alt, we must get out of here! Tell the council we will not get very large. Only enough to disperse this mob. That can do no harm. Togaro knows we are here—if he sees us, what matter? Tell them we'll be small again soon— I'll be ready to go when the flyer is ready."

Alt shouted his translation. The balcony doorway was already shrunk to Drake's waist. He pushed Ahlma through and squeezed through himself with Alt after them.

At sight of them the crowd gave a roar of mingled surprise and fear. The fighting at the palace steps was instantly checked. The crowd stood and gazed. Surprise; awe; terror. It froze them.

There was a total silence. Drake gazed down, and then with a moment of dizziness looked away. The palace was shrinking. He presently reached up and gripped its spire at the peak of the roof. With his other hand drew from his belt pellets of the other drug.

Drake had had much experience with the drugs, each an antidote to the other; he knew how to check his growth at any point. He checked it now, and Ahlma and Alt did the same.

They stood precariously upon a tiny balcony of a toy house whose spire was not much taller than their heads. A few feet beneath them, hardly more than a comfortable step down, was the miniature garden. Little trees, bathed in the blood-light of the moon, and small human figures.

The balcony strained and swayed beneath the weight. Drake said, "We must step down. Alt, call down to them, tell them to give us room."

Alt's voice spurred the crowd to action. The spell which had struck them motionless was broken. A woman screamed. The crowd took it up—frenzied screams. In panic, they turned and shoved, fought, screaming to get away.

But the adjacent streets were packed with people. The crowd from the garden pressed at them.

The balcony was breaking. This toy house; these toy people!

Drake said, "Step down, Ahlma."

There was room beneath them now: They stepped from the balcony, and stood together beside the little palace, with the garden down at their shoe-tops. The crowd in a frenzy was fighting its way back through the trees. There were open spaces in the garden now. Patches of open, blood-red moon-light. But in all of these, motionless tiny figures were lying where they had been trampled.

Contrition swept Drake. It seemed that everything he attempted was doomed to disaster. Ahlma was gripping him.

"Drake, look—off there!"

They could see behind them over the palace roof; the shining lake; the island at the horizon where the Togarites were hiding.

Alt cried out, stricken with horror. And then Drake saw it.

They stood, Drake, Ahlma and Alt, three giants, gazing out over the lake. The dawn was nearer than Drake had realized. The sky above the island was turning red. A bank of clouds off there was reddening. The swift-coming dawn was at hand. The moon was fading. The scene everywhere was brightening.

Upon the island, where a green hill showed dark against the lightening sky, something abnormal showed. A dark shape, growing, expanding. It spread, sidewise and upward; not a human shape, not a giant, but something far more ominous. It was rounded and oblong; and to be visible at this distance it must be already a hundred feet long.

Then in a moment it was twice that. It seemed shoving at the hill with its growth—shoving itself toward the water.

The Togaro spaceship! It had come now suddenly from its hiding place. Realization swept Drake with a surge of horror. Togaro's departure was at hand!

The ship was expanding with tremendous rapidity. It soon had shoved itself off the island with its growth. It lifted slightly and then settled upon the water, floating on a raft-like hull of pontoons.

Another minute. It lay off there as though moored to the tiny island. It was still growing, a monstrous thing now. Most of it was below the curve of the horizon, but its stern loomed up beside the island. A ship a mile long now. In another minute it might be twice that.

Drake's thoughts were whirling. This monstrous thing—why didn't it rise and be gone?

As though to answer his thoughts he became aware that Ahlma and Alt had turned and were gazing again over the city. Then Drake knew why the Togaro vehicle was lingering.

From everywhere about the distant landscape, from a hundred points in the spread of the city, giants were rising! The dawn—this dawn now beginning—was the signal. Giants, widely scattered at various points, appearing now out of smallness!

There was a giant whose head and shoulders rose from one of the city streets quite near at hand. The sight of him caught Drake's fascinated attention. He grew with amazing swiftness to a height of perhaps two hundred feet. Then his growth suddenly stopped. He stood gazing about him. In the faint light of the dawn Drake could see him plainly—a Togarite, stocky, wide-shouldered, bullet-headed. He wore, upon his chest and waist a series of belts. And about his throat a leather necklace, with pads out over his shoulders.

His torso, shoulders and neck were black with clinging tiny human figures! They hung upon his straps like clustering insects. They were in their normal size, Drake judged. They had climbed upon him when he was small. He seemed to be carrying a hundred or more. He stood a moment, then stepped cautiously up to the flat roof of a near-by house. It cracked with his weight. He leaped over it, into another street. He may have crushed scores of people who were gathered there. Drake could hear faint screams. The giant leaped again, found a broader street, ran down it toward the lake, and waded into the water.

A hundred such incidents. A hundred such giants simultaneously appearing at the signal of the dawn. They were carrying ten thousand people at the least. They appeared from everywhere, laden with the tiny clinging figures.

From the distant hills of the open country still more of them came running, dashing through the city, wrecking its houses, trampling the crowds in the streets; heading for the lake.

The water was soon lashed into a turmoil. The giants were all a prearranged height. The water rose only to their hips. It beat white against them as they forced their way through it toward the island where the monstrous vehicle was waiting to receive them.

Drake understood it now. In smallness the Togarites had been secretly working; gathering their followers from among the people. It was an exodus now to the island where the expedition to conquer the earth was ready to depart.

There were giants rising from the island now. More of Togaro's followers, gathered there in smallness, growing now to join this arriving throng of their fellows. One giant, taller than all the others, loomed into the sky, black against the blood-red dawn. He was standing in the lake, far away, so that only his head and shoulders were above the horizon. It may have been Togaro, directing the embarkation. He was monstrous; and the vehicle on the water, lying quiescent now with its stern looming on the curve of the little globe, was monstrous.

The giants were clustered out there, climbing with their human freight into the doorway of the ship. And they were still arriving. The city was wrecked with their passage. The broken streets were littered with mangled forms of the trampled crowds.

The sunrise came. The blurred little sun was red. It bathed the shattered, screaming city with crimson; it painted the running giants; it turned the foaming waters of the lake to blood.

When the turmoil was over and the littered giants had all embarked, off there against the red morning sky the monstrous vehicle was again expanding.

CHAPTER 21

RIDING THE GIANT

I must revert now to that moment when I clung to the huge strap which was the back of Togaro's belt and was lifted through the wrecked cabin of our ship. I could see very little: the bulge of Togaro's shirt above me; the strap of his belt, wide as the length of my arm, to which I clung.

There was a rending crash. A dizzying, monstrous sweep of movement; a thump as we struck the ground; then the rhythmic swoops upward and down which marked Togaro's giant leaps as he ran.

The wind tore past me. I could see the blur of the swaying ground; I seemed at least fifty feet above it. Soon I was higher than that, for Togaro's body was constantly growing.

Then we were in the lake, Togaro wading. The water rose to his hips. It surged in white-lashed waves close under me; the spray from it drenched me. Overhead, fifty feet up or more, I could see one of Dianne's white arms clinging to Togaro's neck. He had evidently given her some of the expanding drug, so that she grew proportionately to him.

I remained tiny. His growth and hers were ended by the time we reached the island. I tried to keep my wits. I was to Togaro the size of an insect now. But if he got smaller he would very soon become aware of me. He stood in the water by the island, looking back at the city. Presently I felt his belt dwindling. I quickly took some of the diminishing drug myself.

We all three dwindled, about maintaining our relative size. The island came up and spread around us. Down into smallness we shrank. I need not detail it. I found that presently we were in a forest of immense green stalks, which might have been grass. They grew gigantic up into the sky. Soon I could only see beside us one monstrous green stalk.

There seemed a sort of ravine in the tumbled, uneven ground. Togaro walked into it. There was a valley. An encampment here!

The encampment of the Togarites on the island! Microscopically small, but Togaro dwindled into it now; and upon his belt I still was clinging.

I saw about me a group of huge dwellings. A crowd of giants. A bustle of activity, making ready for departure. And then I saw the spaceship. It was lying hidden here.

I saw that now Dianne was about the same size as Togaro. He placed her upon the ground; her head towered above my lofty perch. I heard the rumble of Togaro's voice over all the clatter of the camp.

"I will take you aboard, Dianne. We start in two hours."

We went through the ship's doorway. Down a passage, gigantic. Into a cabin, gigantic.

"Dianne, you sit here, quietly, and wait for me. Will you do that? Or are you going to cause me trouble?"

She said, "I am not foolish enough to disobey you, Togaro."

"That is right. I will not hurt you."

There was a cushion on the floor. She sat down. I peered around the bulge of Togaro's waist and saw her. She was looking up at him. Smiling, but it was a pale, harassed smile.

"You speak in English, Togaro? Why is that?"

He faced her; the movement of his turning was a wild swoop through the air for me.

He said, "When I am Master of the Earth it will be our language. We will forget Mita, you and I. This is the end of Mita." His chuckle had an ominous implication. "I will be back presently, Dianne."

I saw that there was a man stationed here at the door of the room on guard. My heart was pounding wildly. Togaro was going out. Above everything I must make my presence known to her. But how could I get down from Togaro's belt? I was fifty feet above the ground.

He walked toward the door. I stood recklessly upon the narrow ledge which was the top thickness of his belt. At the door he stopped to speak to the guard—telling him no doubt to watch Dianne carefully. Togaro's back was toward the cabin wall. A window was here, with a portière and a rope thick as my body. I was swung within a few feet of it. I leaped, caught the rope, wound my legs around it.

I slid cautiously down the fifty-foot length of rope to the ground. I found the floor in shadow. The figure of Dianne was a hundred yards away.

I ran over toward the wall and circled toward her.

CHAPTER 22

"VENGEANCE OF TOGARO!"

To Dianne, and to the guard in the doorway, I was a figure an inch or so in height, plainly to be seen if I moved too fast, or left the shadows of the floor. But I did neither. I reached Dianne safely, though it took me a long time.

I circled behind her. I climbed upon the heights of the cushion, I touched her robe. Did I dare pluck at it? I thought I might perhaps attract her attention.

I took another ten minutes, or it may have been half an hour, climbing along the cushion to its other side. And presently her hand, as she idly moved it, came to rest quite near me. I looked up and saw that her face was turned my way.

I decided to chance it. I darted forward and stood against the curve of her wrist. She felt me. Her instinctive movement of the hand knocked me over, but I fell into the soft billows of the cushion. I lay quiet, praying that she might not cry out.

She recognized me! She made no sound, did not even move. But near me one of her fingers was gently swaying.

I held myself motionless, waiting. In a moment I could feel her turning cautiously, so that her robe might hide me from the guard's view.

A fold of the robe presently came over me like a great golden curtain. Her finger, larger than my body, came carefully feeling for me. I reached for it. Clung to it. It pulled me as it slowly shifted away. And then her thumb came near. I was carefully lifted, carried with a gentle swoop through the air and set down twenty feet away.

A deep shadow was here; I was near the back wall of the cabin. I knew Dianne wanted me to stand quiet; knew that she was planning how we might communicate. Her voice sounded as she spoke to the guard. Their native language—I could not understand it, but quite evidently she was telling him that she was tired, for presently she lay prone, with her head on the cushion.

Her face was turned toward me, and away from the guard. She had made our opportunity. I ran forward. The guard could have seen me then, but he did not, and in a moment Dianne's head was between me and him. I climbed again upon the cushion. I stood beside Dianne's face. Her ear was near me.

"Dianne!"

Her lips moved, whispering, "Yes, Frank!"

"Dianne—I came, riding Togaro. I have the drugs."

"Be very careful, Frank."

I had no conscious plan. I was unarmed now—I had dropped my weapon in the cabin of the other ship when I leaped for Togaro's waist. But there must be some way of getting Dianne out of this room, out of the ship, back to Drake.

"Dianne, do you think if I could get larger and surprise this guard that we could get out?" She had seen more of our surroundings than I.

"No!" She was plainly agitated, but she held herself quiet, just her lips moving in the faintest of whispers. "No! Don't get larger—not now! The passage is full of men—they're loading the ship. We'll be starting soon, Frank, you can escape! Go! Go now—get back to Drake."

"No," I murmured. "Dianne, then you must get small."

"Frank! Run!"

Togaro had returned! I leaped from the cushion and hid near by.

An hour passed. I think it must have been that long. Togaro was talking with Dianne. They spoke in English. He was very gentle with her. He told her they were almost ready to start; told her with triumph that his expedition was larger and in better shape than he had expected.

Dianne knew that father was guarding the rock fragment, and that all these thousands of Togarites could never escape into our earth-world. Togaro knew that also. But he ignored it. Had he a plan perhaps to get his hordes out of the rock?

Dianne was apparently very docile; but I could hear how cautious she was in all she said.

The sounds of the embarkation were constantly audible. Togaro said at last, "I think we are ready."

He went to the door and spoke to the guard. Dianne seized the opportunity to flash me a warning glance.

Togaro came back. "I've ordered the start."

The familiar shock came as the size-changing current suffused the ship. It began enlarging. Togaro took Dianne to the window.

"Stand here, little sweet one."

His tone made me shudder. His arm went around her shoulders. I could see her shrink with repulsion and fear.

"Togaro—"

At once he withdrew his arm. Strange scoundrel! He knew how to handle this girl—or thought he did. He said:

"My silly little Dianne—you almost love me!" He was quizzically ironical. "Almost, but not quite! But that—all in good time I will correct it. Just now we have more important things to worry us."

"Yes," she murmured. "Togaro, you are hurting me."

"Hurting you? I am not touching you!"

"Hurting me—with your threat against my world."

"How strange a way to say it! Hurting you! Which world do you mean I threaten? Why, Dianne, I threaten all worlds!"

He said it boastfully, but with complete irony. "You know that, Dianne. I am as you once told me, the great heartless fiend. The incarnate devil—is that the way you say it in English? The heartless, murderous Togaro. Ah, but not concerning you, little Dianne. My heart is very full of love for you."

She surprised me, and him equally, by retorting vehemently:

"That is a lie! You love yourself—you are in love with your own dream of conquest. Not in love with me! Filled with desire for me? Not very much, Togaro! Enough to make you want to hold me here, amuse yourself with dallying—because you think you are a very great lover. But your greatest desire is to murder! To kill! To destroy your fellow creatures—and you ask me to try to love you."

He put his arm around her again, but she flung him away. He laughed.

"Masterful little woman—a fit mate for Togaro, master of the earth. Would you not say it so, Dianne? You have used all your words and have none left? But if you will not talk, at least you will stand here with me and look out of the window. See, we have come above the island trees now."

They stood silent, gazing. From down by the floor I could see nothing. Then along the wall I noticed where a translucent pane came to the floor to join a floor window. It was dark over there. I ran; and found a jutting edge of casement around which I could peer and see out. It occurred to me that with Togaro and Dianne absorbed, with their backs to the cabin, I might now get large. But the guard had not relaxed.

I stared through the window. We were a gigantic ship now. Our growth was spreading us over the island. I gazed down from a height at the small island trees; they were being mashed beneath us as we grew. The island's hill was near by; we shoved our way at it.

The island was dwindling beneath us. Then Togaro called an order. I could hear the echoes of it being relayed to the control room. The ship lifted; moved away from the tiny island, and settled on the water. I saw on the island some of Togaro's men growing to giants.

The red light of dawn was in the sky. It was the scene Drake, Ahlma and Alt were witnessing as they stood by the palace. Our size-changing current went off. We lay, a monstrous vehicle, with shallow water all around us, and a tiny green island near by.

I heard Togaro say:

"We are not floating, Dianne. See, the water is so shallow, we are grounded upon the bottom. The curve of this little earth is already apparent beneath us—the ends of our ship are in the air."

"Togaro!" His words, the implication of which escaped me then, brought a horror to her. "Togaro, we will depart without getting larger?"

He did not answer, he merely laughed and said, "Wait and see, Dianne. Look now; my loyal followers are arriving."

The giants, clustered with their tiny human freight, came wading. They stood in the lashed blood-red waters; then came aboard.

The ship resounded with the turmoil of their arrival. They thronged the corridors; their tiny human burdens were taken from them and herded like ants into the various cabins. One of the giants, still littered, came to our door and spoke to Togaro. I saw him as a fellow about Togaro's own height. The people he was carrying were as small as I now was myself. He presently turned and went away.

The embarkation proceeded. For ten minutes or so, Togaro left Dianne and went outside. He commanded her to stay by the window; and with the guard doubly watchful, she obeyed.

Nor did I move. I saw Togaro outside, standing in the water. His figure grew so monstrous beside the ship that only the lower part of his legs was visible. He was searching the horizon, no doubt, to make sure that no more of his men were coming. Then, after a moment, he was dwindling. He came aboard in his former size.

"All are aboard, little Dianne. We are ready to make the final start."

She said, with a frightened hush to her voice: "Start away in space, Togaro?"

"No!" he said grimly. "We shall stay here, Dianne, resting upon the curve of your little world—and grow a little larger. Why not?"

She could find no words. He added, "We're leaving this world Mita forever, Dianne."

She burst out, with more anger than horror this time—but I knew it was a pretended anger, and that horror was sweeping her. "Why not, indeed! Bring death here to no purpose—why not?"

"I'll tell you," he said: "I would have ruled your world, with you as my queen. Your people would not have me. Rejected me—made me an outcast. Now they shall pay for it!"

He said it with a horrible, calm grimness. "Pay for it, Dianne, by dying! Death at the hand of Togaro. Vengeance of Togaro. Ten million people die, because Togaro is angry!"

It struck her silent; she stood white and silent and helpless beside him. And as though Fate were determined to keep me helpless also, the guard at the door stood with renewed alertness, his gaze searching the room.

CHAPTER 23

DOOMED LITTLE PLANET!

The last scenes upon the planet Mita, as it was given to me to witness them, were unfolded now beyond this window through which I was gazing. I suppose it took another hour. It might have been far longer.

Tremendous fearsome drama! I saw, far below this window, a toy lake—a scene in miniature of a lake with little green islands. I must have been near the stern of the ship. Looking down, I could see that our tremendous hull was jutting into the air, high above the water. Our growth had pushed us back toward the city at the lakeshore. I saw the city now come into view beneath me.

A brief glimpse. It was full daylight. Our hull was jutting a thousand feet perhaps above the tiny houses. I saw the wrecked and littered streets where the giants had passed.

The glimpse of a minute or two, no more. But what I saw down there is stamped with indelible horror upon my memory. It was a city of wild confusion, black with surging, tiny people, trampling over the dead and dying unheeded. Fires broke out in the shattered buildings. The great black shadow of our looming hull overhead lay for a moment like a finger of death upon the scene. In the gloom down there, the fires showed lurid yellow and red, with black smoke rising in tiny wisps.

A minute, then the scene had dwindled and passed beneath us beyond my sight. Our hull did not touch the city; upon this shrinking little globe—this surface becoming every moment more visibly convex—we were balanced amidships somewhere off in the lake, with the curving world falling away from under our bow and stern.

My window soon was high above a toy landscape of miniature forests and scattered dwellings; and ribbons of roads. There seemed people running along the roads.

A line of mountains showed; the sunset was on them; and to one side I could see a curving ocean. All shrinking—small, but sharp and clear in every detail as though I were gazing through a diminishing glass.

The mountains came down under me. The sunlight faded from them; beyond them I saw the stars.

I heard Togaro give an order. Our ship lifted a trifle and hung poised. The sharply curving landscape lowered. Then, with a gasp I realized how monstrously large we had become. Why this was the top of a little globe beneath me! It was not far away—only a few miles down; but it was so small that I could see all the curve of its upper surface—all the configurations of land and water; and the stars gleaming beyond it. A little ball, hanging here in space close under me. Its entire diameter was not much longer now than the hull-length of our ship.

Another few minutes. The scene from an earthly landscape, was turning celestial. We were in space. Black space, with blazing, glittering stars. Mita's sun was visible—a fiery globe with a vivid corona of mounting flames. Still, close under us, the planet Mita, like a child's ball, hung attached to us by gravitation.

The heavens were visibly rotating. We clung to Mita, so that the rotating planet carried us around. We were a monstrous weight, larger than the planet now, but still gravitationally attached to it. I could fancy the planet lurching. Its axial rotation lurching wildly. Its orbital swing about its little sun suddenly altered.

We rose presently and swung away from Mita. The sun was over my head—I could not see it. But beneath me I saw the planet. A ball—like a ball of steel magnetized, following a monstrous magnet. It followed us. It clung to our giant bulk, with the force of gravity irresistibly drawing it after us.

Now all my vague understanding of Togaro's purpose burst upon me with full realization. We were swooping toward Mita's little sun! A moment, and then the ship echoed with Togaro's vehement commands. We swung away from the sun. With speed and size gigantic, we swooped sidewise and darted away.

My window showed celestial space. But I saw how small it was! Distant tiny stars, all disturbed, chaotic with this giant bulk of our ship come among them! The sun and Mita were close to us, directly before my window. A ball of yellow-red blazing gases, and a little lurching planet!

We had shaken Mita off, flung it like a pitched ball. Upon that side of our hull we were repulsive now to gravity. Mita's orbital revolution about its sun was checked. It staggered—and then began falling.

A slow movement at first. I stared. Then I could see the movement: a crazily spinning little ball, lurching, falling—

Doomed little planet, falling toward its flaming sun!

CHAPTER 24

THE END OF A WORLD

I have from Drake his impressions of those last hours on Mita. A wild, chaotic picture his memory holds. Jumbled impressions—yet as I record them in that fashion, doubtless I will approximate the truth, for they were jumbled, frantic scenes of panic—millions of people struggling upon a doomed world!

Upon Drake there was a sense of despair; his own futility was so clearly shown, and the futility of his plans! He had sent Alt to have me come into the atom with automatics. He stood before Dianne's palace, gazing at a world gone mad. An automatic was in his hand, as futile as a cap pistol in the hands of a child.

By nature Drake was resourceful; cautious, but reckless too, when he thought reckless daring was necessary. He stood, there as a giant with Ahlma and Alt, and saw in the blood-red dawn Togaro's monstrous vehicle expanding into the sky. It did not need Alt's horrified words to bring realization to Drake; nor the wrecked city—the turmoil of the panic-stricken throngs—to make Drake realize that this was the end. He knew it.

A very human sense of utter failure made Drake stand and tell himself bitterly that there was no use trying to do anything. But the feeling passed. It is instinctive to struggle for life against every most desperate circumstance. Drake became aware that in the wrecked city spread there in the dawn before him, thousands of people were struggling for life. Doing nothing with any rational thought—and yet struggling.

Behind him, in the palace, he heard the shouts of the councilmen; the clatter of footsteps. The government, against all these odds, was striving to do something. Nobody was quitting.

It stung him into action.

"Alt, we must get back to normal size! Help them, Alt. This is death if we stand here."

They took the drug. The scene dwindled. The Togaro ship off there on the water seemed rising to new gigantic proportions. Its huge stern was coming toward the city. Projecting above the water now; Drake could see the space between the bottom of its hull and the lake surface. It came, that giant stern, shoving its way forward. The length of its hull extended like a gray wall off for miles to the horizon where it lay balanced, with other miles on beyond, the shape of it blurred by distance against the red sky of dawn.

Drake attained normal size. Ahlma clung to him.

Alt, too, was struggling to cope with a terror almost overpowering. "Drake—what—what can we do?"

They were down in the garden now, at the doorway of the palace. Officials were running in and out. Calling orders, with no one to hear them. Some of the police stood here, inactive, stupefied with terror.

"Come inside," said Drake. He pulled at the confused Alt. "Don't you understand? Our ship may be repaired by now. We've got to get it repaired! Herd the people into it! Make it large enough to take us all—all these people. Alt, we've got to send messengers—send them in giant size—to the other cities! The local airships—dispatch them to bring the people here—get them all into our vehicle and get away! You understand? This is the end of the world here! Abandon it! This is—the end!"

They ran into the turmoil of the palace.

In the chaos of those final hours Drake must have played a leading and a masterful part. He does not tell it so, but I think it is true. Authority—the routine of any official activity—was wholly gone. Of them all, it was Drake who held most of his wits, who gave orders and enforced obedience.

The time was very short. There was an hour—or even less—while the red dawn faded into full light of day. The monstrous hull of the Togaro ship projected like a black roof over all the scene. The shadow of it lay black upon the city, the palace and lake. It grew until up there in the sky nothing else could be seen.

Then it lifted. It moved up a few miles. It hovered up there. From one horizon to the other it loomed, a solid dark shape like a leaden cloud-bank. Its great pontoons were visible. The rectangles of floor windows showed in its bulging hull.

An expanding dark cloud. It soon was spread so wide that all across the sky was only one small section of its length—one pontoon, one window.

But during that hour Drake was accomplishing things in all the turmoil of people almost stricken of reason by terror. The spaceship was ready at last. The repairs fortunately had been almost finished before the panic began.

Messengers were sent into the burning city with orders to herd the crowd to the landing field. Local ships were sent to other cities. Some got started, some did not. But a few, at the very last, came back loaded with refugees. The young men of that army which Drake had expected to lead into smallness against Togaro, were now most useful of all. They understood the drugs and could be trusted with them. In the lower room of the palace Drake stood with the main supply of drugs. He dealt them out to this little army. A hundred or more. They stood, white-faced and silent; but alert, eager to obey.

"Alt, tell them—" Drake cursed his inability to speak with any fluency this native language. But Alt, always at his elbow, was swift to interpret. "Alt, tell these ten to get large, very large, and run to the water city."

Another ten, somewhere else; and others. In a size gigantic, they could circle this little globe on foot in an hour or so. They were to pick up as many of the people as possible and bring them back.

The lower room of the palace was dark now. The brief day was past. Night had come. Stars, and the moon. But the moon had only shown for a moment. The black cloud, the shape of the Togaro vehicle, was up there among the stars. The moon had swung crazily and was gone.

Into the palace windows came the mingled sounds of the night of chaos: screams, the roaring of futile orders in the garden, where a crowd was surging over the trampled neglected bodies. Darkness out there, painted by the lurid glare from the burning city.

Drake dispatched his men. They turned out into the frantic night, fought their way for space in the milling throngs, and took their drug. Soon they were rising as giants, moving cautiously to the open country, then running.

Drake had been to the landing field several times. The vehicle was ready. It lay gigantic, spreading all across the field. Thousands of refugees were in it. Others were momentarily arriving. Ten thousand now, the officials there told Drake. A thousand, hurt in the throngs or crushed by the passing of Togaro's giants, had also been carried here.

Drake sent the other men to search the city—to bring back from the littered streets any who seemed still alive. From the palace gardens and the nearest streets, the police were spurred to carry in the maimed.

A thousand people arrived while Drake stood there on the field. A local ship came down and landed with another thousand. Two of his men, gigantic, came dashing up with another thousand clinging to them whom they had collected in the near-by rural sections. Men and women, and children huddled in their parents' arms. Some had bundles of clothes, which for all this clinging to the back of a giant in the last hours of the end of a world they still were reluctant to abandon. Families, trudging aimlessly along country roads in the night or driving carts piled with household treasures, had been seized by these friendly giants and brought to the vehicle.

A lump was in Drake's throat. These few thousands of people, arriving here to what might or might not be ultimate safety—but there were ten million people here on this doomed little world!

Drake wondered how long he dared hold the vehicle here. The night itself was wildly crazy. He saw the moon vanish with a lunge. The stars were abnormally swaying. A wind was springing up from the lake, a violent, aimless wind. The water lashed against the shore.

The arriving giants reported storms in the other hemisphere. The sea had mounted and submerged many of the islands.

Then the next dawn came. The sun swung crazily up. Swiftly, abnormally mounting to the zenith. And there, against all reason of nature, it seemed to hang motionless; for an hour perhaps. Then it dropped visually sidewise, and came again, swaying like a pendulum.

The Togaro vehicle showed only occasionally now as a distant blur among the stars. Mita was wildly lurching. This was not day and night. A chaos!

Drake knew it was near the end. The sun presently hung motionless. It was growing hotter. Its heat and fiercely intensified light beat down. Soon they would be intolerable.

"A few hours more, Alt. That's all we can stay here."

Drake was horribly worried over Ahlma. She had pleaded:

"I am experienced with the drug. You must let me go, Drake. Let me get large—I will bring some of them back to safety—"

In his harassed activity he had yielded, had stood watching her huge robed figure running off into the night. She had not yet returned. A hundred times he had felt that he must drop everything and go after her. But he could not be spared; nor could he spare Alt.

Twice Drake had checked the embarking multitude and had ordered the vehicle to grow larger. It lay now across the field and over half a dozen near-by city streets. They had been cleared of people, and the growing vehicle had crushed the houses there into a wreckage of masonry.

The end was near. The sun was twice its normal size. The glaring heat was horrible. Jain, with other officials, were demanding the start.

"No! Not yet!" But Drake knew that not for very long could he force his way.

A few giants were still straggling in; Drake and Alt and a hundred other leaders were standing in a giant size at the vehicle doorway. The glare of sunlight was blinding. The lake was roaring with a hot, sulphurous wind plucking at it, lashing it.

But Ahlma had not come. Then off over the toy landscape, Drake saw the blur of her robe. Her head and shoulders mounted above the horizon. She came running with great leaps. As she arrived Drake saw the small figures upon her. Women and children, almost all of them.

"Ahlma!" He was her own size. He touched her; words would not come. But he knew that the safety of all these multitudes had meant less to him than the life of this one girl.

"Ahlma, go in. They'll unload them inside—There—the doorway—"

"Yes, Drake. How many are here?"

"We think about a hundred and ten thousand."

"Oh!"

It was so few, out of ten million!

Ahlma went into the ship. Drake turned to Jain. "Shall we start?"

"We must!"

A toy world lay wrecked at their feet. Clouds had come suddenly down. They swirled over the land—tumbling black mist, shot with lurid green and turgid yellow. But the sun beat through them. Rain had came in a downpour; but the sun beat it away and dried it up.

"Come in then, Jain."

No, there was another giant coming. He panted up with his cluster of refugees. And then another came.

They could wait no longer. There was a moment when no arriving giants were in sight. Ten million people on this doomed planet—only a few over a hundred thousand were here to depart. But the sun was too hot. The scene was strewn with people who had fallen in the heat. Drake was suddenly staggering. Jain pulled at him, and the door closed after them. From a stricken toy world, the vehicle struggled away.

The interior of the ship was a blur of murmuring sounds. A hundred or so giants, like Drake, to whom the ship was a thing a few hundred feet long; and a hundred and ten thousand people, small as ants, swarming it everywhere.

Drake stood at a window. He thinks he must have stood there for hours. The surface of Mita dropped away as the ship sped off into space. The stars showed, celestial space.

The Togaro vehicle was gone. Drake saw Mita through his window. A little ball. The sun lighted it upon one side, so that it showed as a reddish half moon, with the dark portion dimly visible.

Drake's ship was expanding. But after an hour or so its size-changing mechanism was shut off. It hovered—the Mitans in control of it lingering with fascinated gaze to witness the destruction of their world.

It took perhaps a few hours more. Mita was falling. The yellow-red ball of sun hung off there in the black field of space beneath Drake's window. Mita seemed above, falling slowly. The movement was hardly visible at first. But it accelerated. The two bodies visibly drawing together.

Then Mita was rushing. Drake thinks he remembers seeing a tail streaming out behind it. A tail, like a comet, as though by its fall it were turning incandescent and leaving a stream of glowing star-dust. Or perhaps with its rapid fall, its atmosphere was leaving it—dust-laden air streaming off into space where the dust caught the sunlight and glowed. There is no one to say.

A fall of millions of miles. It was that far, to Mita. I can fancy, in those last hours, the blazing heat withering everything upon the planet's surface. Its ten million inhabitants—save those few Drake had helped to rescue—I can think that long before the end, they were dead; shriveled, fallen in the heat. Smothered, choked by the gasses which must have polluted what little atmosphere was left.

Drake saw the end. The planet plunged. Fell like a plummet at the last and struck the blazing surface of its sun. There was a flash; a leaping, extra spurt of flame for just a moment in the sun's corona.

Then the sun blazed alone. What had been Mita was fused and gone. Non-existent!

From the window Drake turned shudderingly away. He had seen the end of a world.

CHAPTER 25

IN THE CAMPFIRE LIGHT

There were some forty thousand people on the Togarite ship, adventuring out upon the conquest of the earth. A few hundred men, who were the Togarite leaders. I think there were perhaps six or eight hundred of these in all. They were experienced with the drugs, and constituted Togaro's active army.

Not very many for the conquest of all the nations of our earth. Yet enough! I realized it as I contemplated what they could do. Togaro was planning carefully. There were thousands of other men on this ship—Mitans who had joined his cause. He could easily have trained them. But he was wise enough to realize that the diabolical power of the drugs needed always to be kept under his close control. He could handle his six or eight hundred trusted men; a larger army might have been awkward.

There were several hundred giants aboard the ship now. The rest of the horde was in a tiny size. They had no drugs. They were men—but there were women and children also. I could imagine that all the renegades of Togaro's world were assembled here, eager with the lust of conquest of an earth they had never seen.

They swarmed the vehicle now. They were as small as I. Fortunately none came to this cabin where Dianne was closely watched, and where I was lurking. If they had come, being so small, they would doubtless have discovered me.

I did not dare leave the cabin; nor did I find, during all the voyage which lasted what seemed twenty-four hours perhaps, an opportunity of again communicating with Dianne.

I need not detail this outward voyage. I saw many strange things through that cabin window. The reverse of the inward trip. Diminishing, shrinking space. The stars becoming so small that they flared about us like a rain of sparks.

Great voids of distance, always shrinking. Then at last, the gray glowing molecules. Whirling and tumbling. A few at first, very far away. Then many, very close. Then great clouds of them, rolling and swirling. Dark. But sometimes shimmering. And always shrinking—congealing into solidity.

The transitions from one condition to another—from celestial space to solid, rocky abyss—were never apparent, and impossible of close description. I was watching eagerly for solidity. I did not see it come—I saw only that at last it was there—out there in the void. A vague, distant rocky wall. It dropped downward, as though we were mounting. Barren cliffs gigantic, but dwindling. Closing in upon us.

Activity became apparent throughout the ship as we neared the voyage end. Dianne, after a few hours, had been given into the charge of several giant women. She had been taken away to another cabin. A wild thought came to me that I should cling to her robe. But the thing had come suddenly, unexpectedly. I was across the cabin. I could not reach her; the chances of discovery would have been too great. I lay in a recess niche of the bottom of the wall, and watched her go.

Later I found upon the floor some crumbs of food which she had dropped for me. They were, to my size, great chunks of a baked dough, like bread. I ate part of them. My hunger was appeased, but I suffered from thirst.

Togaro used this cabin now for consultation with some of his men. I lay, carefully hidden. The room was brighter than before, and the guard was constantly alert. Togaro sat at a table with a few of his men around him.

They talked in their native language; I could not understand a word of it. He seemed to be planning his campaign. He had lived in our world for a year. He doubtless knew a good deal about it. He spread upon the table now what seemed to be maps.

The ship landed in the depths of a stunted forest. Dark, shadowed verdure, with a dim effulgence of light upon far distant mountain ranges. The disembarkation took an hour or more. I could hear the people marching out of the ship, clustering in the forest, setting up their first encampment with the giants helping them. There seemed no need for secrecy. Fires began springing up. Portable houses of animal skins, like tents, were erected. Meals were prepared. A myriad duties necessary to the welfare of forty thousand people were under way.

I climbed through the wire-woven side hull of the ship, and reached the ground safely. I stood beside a tree. The giant ship had mangled a great spread of the forest. I found that I had got out none too soon. The ship began shrinking. Its crew was taking it into a smaller size, to hide it—or abandon it somewhere—and then themselves return to rejoin the encampment. It dwindled, and presently was gone. The mashed forest trees lay like broken jackstraws where it had been.

I stood for perhaps an hour there in the darkness, getting my bearings upon these new conditions. I was about normal in size to this forest; this tree was stunted, but its limbs arched out over me for what seemed twenty or thirty feet.

I found, too, that these thousands of people encamped here over several miles of forest territory, were all about my size. And the giants now began dwindling. Evidently they found it dangerous to move about—difficult to avoid trampling the tiny multitude. They dwindled to the smaller stature.

It was presently almost a normal earthly scene. A forest encampment by night. Camp fires of burning brush; cone-shaped tents; like wigwams; families clustered over their outdoor meal; the Togarite leaders giving orders, directing the activity.

I did not see Togaro himself. Nor Dianne. I would have to move about and locate her. I pondered changing size. It did not seem advisable. With a smaller stature I could not, in days, tramp about this camp and find Dianne. Or if now I got larger, I would be instantly conspicuous. I was conspicuous enough already. My garments were different from all these Mitans—my knitted bathing suit marked me for a stranger. My whole aspect—my language—differed.

I made a start. I moved cautiously off through the trees. The lights from the fires were circles of red and yellow. I kept out of them, in the recessed shadows. Somewhere, at one of these fires, Dianne must be sitting. I wondered if I could locate Togaro; he might have Dianne with him.

Occasionally figures passed near me. I was seen no doubt, but only dimly. Once I almost bumped into a man who was gathering brushwood. A woman and a child came up and took it from him. I mumbled something and ducked away.

The incident gave me an idea. The man was garbed in a jacket with puffed, flaring sleeves and a circular bottom that flared like a skirt at his knees. And he wore a cone-shaped hat, broad-brimmed. It was a costume distinctive, and characteristic of most of these men. If I could get possession of such a jacket and hat, they would disguise me.

I wandered on, skulking the fringes of the camp like a lurking Indian in a primitive American forest.

The camp finally settled to sleep. The fires died. The Togarite men patrolled back and forth, silent shadows in the gloom.

I found my opportunity at last. A tent, where by the embers of a fire outside a man's jacket and hat were lying. I watched my chance when no guard was near. I darted forward, seized the garments and made away.

Shrouded by the jacket, hiding my belt of drugs, with the hat brim pulled low over my eyes, I felt a measure of security. I realized that I was exhausted—that all during the outward voyage I had hardly dared relax to sleep. I found now a wooded glen of ferns, dark and secluded, with a blessed little rill of water at which I slaked my burning thirst.

Then I lay down, and in a moment was sleeping heavily.

The sound of voices wakened me. People were passing near me, but they did not see me. Or if they did, my sleeping form caused no comment. How long I had slept I did not know. But I was again hungry. And I found that the camp was fully awake, bustling with its morning duties.

Morning? The darkness was no different from before. The camp fires were lighted again. All that day—if day it could be called—I skulked, an outcast in the encampment, stealing what food I needed. I found that my aspect, unless under too close a scrutiny, was passing unnoticed.

But I could not locate Dianne or Togaro. There were forty thousand people here in the forest. I skulked from one fire to another, but without success.

Had Dianne been taken away? Again I cursed myself for an inept fool. I wondered how long Togaro intended to keep this encampment? Then presently I realized what was being done. I saw near by, in a clearing, a giant rising. He grew to what looked like several hundred feet, and then stopped. A gathered throng was off there, and I made my way in that direction.

The tents were struck here. A thousand people were ready to start away. The giant was giving them the drug. They marched off as they started growing, with the giant leading them—dim figures towering into the immensity of distance until presently they had vanished.

I realized now how this multitude would be taken upward into largeness. There was not a sufficient supply of the drug for them all to have it at a small size. The single Togarite captain, getting large, expanded his drugs and then fed the thousand people in his charge; at every stage of the journey he would do the same.

There were parties such as this starting now at regular intervals. I wandered on; and I found Dianne at last. It was again near the time of sleep. Ten thousand of the people had departed—but thirty thousand were still here awaiting their turn.

Dianne was seated at a camp fire, around which several women were cooking a meal. A tent stood near by—a peaked canopy of skins. It was larger than most of the others, with tasseled drapings at its doorway. Dianne's tent, where she was waited upon by these women, I did not doubt.

I stood in the shadows of a tree, just outside the circle of fire light. The light of the playing logs made Dianne's golden robe glisten; etched her sharply against the darkness behind her. She sat composed and quiet, with a regal dignity as the women prepared to serve her. I thought, as I stood there in the darkness, that I had never seen her so beautiful.

Could I get to her? I saw that for all her composed casual manner, she was very alert.

I stood planning. A smaller size for me alone was not practical—I had tried that before. But now, concealed under my jacket was enough of the diminishing drug for both her and me. If I could get to her unchallenged, she and I could take the drug and escape into smallness.

Whatever chance I had was at once gone. Togaro appeared! In a size normal to Dianne and me, he came sauntering up to her fire and greeted her. He was broadly smiling, evidently in a high good humor. He wore a vivid outer jacket; his whole aspect—the colored sash about his hips, his tasseled leggings—was that of a cavalier in jaunty, debonair mood.

I saw that he had discarded his belt of drugs. He took off his circular hat and cast it to the ground.

The meal was ready. Togaro evidently dismissed the women; they moved back, out of my line of vision behind the tent. I heard his voice saying in English:

"You will serve us, little Dianne. Why not? A supper here together, before we start the upward trip."

I could not hear what she said, but he answered:

"Yes, tonight. When we have eaten, Dianne. I have everything organized—I am not needed here. You and I and your serving maids will start. The next camp will be ready ahead of us—it will not be too long a journey." He laughed. "I would not tire my little Dianne. I am good to you; can you say it that I am not?"

I stood tense. To follow them upward would be difficult. It was now or never.

Dianne moved about, serving the meal. They sat down facing each other beside the fire and began to eat. Dianne was as yet wholly unaware of my presence. I edged a little closer, slipped from one tree to another until I was behind Togaro, with Dianne facing me.

I stood now in the darkness beside the bole of a tree, just beyond the circle of fire light. I was hardly twenty feet from them. I could hear their voices. My foot touched a loose rock. I stooped and picked it up—a chunk larger than my fist. I thought that there might be no one watching the scene. I wanted to creep forward, cross the lighted area, and strike Togaro before he could make an outcry.

But Dianne must be made aware of me first, to be on her guard and ready for my rush.

I took a step forward. She would see me now, I hoped—see me as a vague, shadowy form in the gloom. I took off my hat, and got the diminishing drug quickly available. I stood tense, gripping the chunk of rock, a finger of my other hand to my lips warning her to silence. If she would see me, she must have the presence of mind not to start, or make any sign that would warn Togaro.

I thought I saw her stiffen. She stared my way.

"Togaro—"

It made my heart leap wildly. Was she about to call his attention to my lurking figure? Did she see me, but not recognize me?

She stammered, "Togaro—you know I hate you. But hate and love are very close. I—was wondering why you put on that sash. It's very becoming."

She had recognized me! I could not miss it—I even fancied she had sent me a warning glance. But she looked instantly away, smiling now with a mocking allure upon Togaro.

She leaned toward him. She repeated, "I hate you, Togaro," exactly as before, yet with a great difference.

Though I knew it was deception, it shot a pang through me nevertheless; and it must have struck at Togaro with a surge of emotion. Whatever alertness to his surroundings he had had was gone. He put out a hand and seized her by the shoulder. "Hate me? Why—"

She swayed toward him and was in his arms. But she struggled a little.

"Togaro, how dare you! Don't you dare—"

There is no man who can yield up a woman when she struggles like that. I thought that over his shoulder she had shot me another glance.

I darted forward. Dianne was fighting with Togaro. Playfully—but she saw me coming, and she changed. Gripped him by the face, with one of her small hands over his mouth. Then she lunged, flung herself upon him. The attack knocked him sidewise. He fell upon one arm.

For an instant she held her hand over his mouth against all his surprised effort to tear it away. In that instant I was upon them. I did not dare fling the rock.

Togaro saw me coming. With a lunge he cast off Dianne, and half rose to meet me. We went down together. He was far stronger than I; and though I landed on top of him, he rolled me over.

I was aware of Dianne plucking at us, striving to impede Togaro as we fought.

The rock was still in my hand, but Togaro had my arm pinned. He fought silently, then he let out a bellow. The camp took it up, and the uproar surged toward us.

I was underneath him, and his hands went to my throat. But that released my arm. I struck upward with the chunk of rock. It must have hit him a glancing blow on the head. He relaxed; slumped, a dead weight upon me.

I squirmed out from under him.

"Frank, this way!"

Dianne seized me. The alarm was spreading over all this section of the camp. Men were running toward us. We dashed away into the trees.

"Wait—here, take this, Dianne."

We took the drug; ran on through the underbrush, dodging the firelight. The scene expanded. The shouting in the camp faded into a dim muffled roar overhead, and then was gone.

CHAPTER 26

THE BLACK AND WHITE FLAGS

"It Seems so strange, Dianne, our being alone together."

"Strange, Frank?" Her laugh was like the pealing of little fairy bells. "Strange? Why, when we were children we were together nearly all the time."

Six years now since I had been alone with Dianne. She had been my sister. We were alone now in the abyss—I was very conscious of how alone we were. We sat by a rock, resting. We had found a pool of water. This was our first stopping since we had escaped from Togaro.

We had no food, but we felt that we could get out of the rock fragment to father before the need of it would be serious. We had encountered no Togarites. This vast abyss—these endless mountains, cañons and caverns of rock—seemed able to hold friends and enemies innumerable, and yet never force them together.

We had at first got small enough to escape from the Togarite encampment; had run, cautiously making our size larger so that the running would take us an appreciable distance from the camp. Once away from immediate pursuit, we started our upward journey in earnest.

We had soon found ourselves lost. It was all a strange, desolate, unknown region to me. But Dianne had traveled it before; as we grew larger, the main configurations of the dwindling region became familiar to her. She found a route different from that which the Togarite expedition had proposed using.

Discussing it with Dianne, I found myself puzzled at her confidence in finding her way out and still avoiding the Togarite parties who were ahead of us. Strange physical conditions, those of this size-change traveling! Yet a moment's thought made the matter clear.

Traveling inward—becoming small—the slightest deviation from the true direction would lead the traveler into vast new realms. Countless universes spreading at his feet. There was space here, limitless. In the size we were when upon Mita there was around us in just that single atom countless light-years of astronomical distance. Coming back, we left the atom. It shrank to a microscopical point. We grew larger than the atoms; larger than the molecules.

Space within this fragment of rock which father was guarding was constantly shrinking. Yet even in the abyss of the Togarite camp it was a vast space. I cannot calculate it. But envisaging the distance from one side of the rock fragment to the other, let us call it a thousand miles.

We grew still larger. Soon, to us, there would be only five hundred miles of distance in here. Then one hundred. Then one mile. Then only a few feet, until at last we would emerge and see that all the space had shrunk to the size of our hand.

Thus, coming out, all roads led in very nearly the same direction. There was no solidity to the rock when viewed from the smaller viewpoint; there is, indeed, no solidity to anything. A growing body, avoiding being crushed, would at last emerge, no matter in what direction it went.

Do I make it clear? I hope so.

At last we stopped, between the drug doses, to rest. We were at the bottom of a vast circular caldron. Tumbled crags strewn in heaps. The opposite rim, some ten miles away, was dimly visible in the gloom. There were shadows in here now; it seemed that overhead a vague sheen of light was apparent. We were near the top. Soon we would be out. I touched Dianne's hand.

"You think we're larger—ahead of all the Togarites now?"

"Yes, I think so."

I did, also. It was imperative that we get out of the rock first, get up there and warn father what was coming. If we did that, the expanding Togaro hordes wouldn't have a chance.

"We'll have to rig up a black and white flag as a signal to father. You remember, Dianne? I told you I'd arranged that with him. But how the deuce can we?"

She surprised me by drawing from her robe a square of white fabric with black stripes upon it.

"Dianne!"

"I found a chance to make it, Frank—on the ship when Togaro sent me to another cabin."

She displayed it proudly. "Is it all right?"

It certainly was. A flag about two feet square. I stood up now and spread it out.

"We'll wave it—like this, Dianne. Father will see it when we're still very small."

I showed her how we'd wave it.

"Frank! Stop!"

Her gaze was off across the dim abyss of the caldron.

"Over there, Frank! Do you see something moving? I do!"

Miles away, partly up the opposite cliffside of the caldron, it seemed that something was moving. The light was very dim, yet distant objects were unnaturally sharp and clear. Something moving off there. We stared. Then we thought we saw human figures standing on that far-off cliff, and something waving.

"A flag, Frank!"

It seemed a flag. A black and white flag, something like our own, waving at us!

The space-voyage which Drake, Ahlma, and Alt made from the doomed planet, was very similar to this one I had just taken on the Togaro ship. The Mitans landed in the abyss of rock. A hundred miles, or a thousand, from the Togarite camp? There is no one to judge.

It was a full day, perhaps, after Togaro landed. A similar scene of activity ensued, save that nearly three times as many people were here; unorganized, badly equipped, refugees struggling upward, not bent upon conquest, seeking only safety.

The voyage had been a busy one for Drake. He had tried to organize things. There was not enough food or enough of the expanding drug for this multitude. Drake organized it into smaller divisions, each in charge of one of the Mitan officials.

When they landed, and the ship was hidden, the refugees began moving upward in size, the leader of each party going ahead with food and drugs, expanding them and dealing them out to his people.

It was the same system that Togaro was using. A slow journey upward, stopping at each stage to erect a new encampment.

And immediately upon disembarking, Mitan leaders were sent out as scouts—alert to locate the Togarites, and to avoid them.

In the first encampment Drake sat in consultation with Jain.

"I think, Jain, this is the best we can do. Get part way up—get all the people up to that size—and then wait."

There was room down here to avoid the Togarites. But farther up in the dwindling space a clash would be inevitable.

"You wish to go ahead of us?"

"Yes, with Alt and Ahlma. They know the way. We will take this black and white flag." (Ahlma had made a flag.) "We can travel fast, Jain. We'll go out and see my father. He controls everything up above. The Togarites can't get out—and if we keep away from them, we're safe enough. No use killing any of our Mitan people by fighting down in here."

"But what about us?" Jain demanded with a touch of suspicion.

"I'll come back to you, Jain. Warn my father that this Togarite horde may try to make a rush out, or get out by trickery. Warn him—and make arrangements so that he can distinguish you Mitans from the Togarites. Then, in small parties, we will go out."

Drake, Ahlma, and Alt started upon their journey. They went swiftly. Thousands of miles, perhaps, from Dianne and me at the beginning. Like us, they got safely ahead of the Togarites. At one stage they sighted a Togaro party, but managed to avoid and pass it without being discovered.

The dwindling space near the top brought them in our vicinity. They were standing on the caldron rim, and saw our black and white flag as I tentatively waved it for Dianne. They waved their own.

We were cautious approaching one another, each suspecting an enemy ruse. But we came together at last.

Reunion! The five of us here, with all the Togarites presumably behind us; and father and the safety of our blessed earth close overhead. It seemed, with Drake and Alt here with me—with Ahlma and Dianne babbling news of what had happened to each other—that all our dangers were at an end. It was an inexpressible relief.

We grew out of the caldron into the space above, the huge familiar valley. I remembered it; but it seemed rather darker now than it had been before.

With our flags out, we stood expanding. Above this valley was the upper surface of the rock fragment. Once we got up there to the summit, father would see us. I wondered if he would be on guard. Or Foley? Or the other man—Ransome—whom we employed? It had only been a few days since Alt and I left here. Days? The events which had crowded them made them seem months to my memory.

The valley shrank and closed in upon us. A pit now.

"Drake, shall we climb out? Or wait a little longer?"

It seemed best for us to start climbing. It was no more than a hundred feet up. Easy enough, with us three men to help the girls.

We scrambled up the rocky slope. We were halfway up when it had dwindled so that the upper rim was barely ten feet above us. There was light up there, and vague, blurred shadows of form in the hazy sky.

"Jump, Dianne. Here, I've got you."

We scrambled out of the closing pit, and stood a moment expanding upon the upper surface. Jagged rock spires were around us, a broken area of crags upon the summit of the rock. A few acres up here, and down over an abyss was the surface of the granite slab.

The scene shrank further, and then the last drug we had taken ceased its action. We stood on a narrow, jagged peak of rock. A slope led down beside us to a broad, undulating plain. It was only ten feet down.

Alt stood with the girls. Drake and I were together, waving our flags. We saw things dimly at first—the brighter light up here confused us.

"Frank, you think he sees us?"

"What is that, off there?"

There was something very strange here! A chill swept over me. Drake was not familiar with the surroundings father and I had prepared for the guarding of the rock, but I was. This seemed a very strange scene now!

Words choked me. I stood clutching Drake.

"What is it, Frank—what's the matter?"

This light overhead was not the light father and I had rigged up! There was no giant microscope up there in the sky.

Vague blurred shapes of a ceiling and wall were up there, and a light— but not our light in the guarded room of our house at King's Cove.

This vast plain, gleaming dimly rough and undulating in the light—it should have been our granite slab. But it was not!

Realization surged over me with a chilling rush of horror. This was a different room. There were people here; I heard an echoing rumble of their giant voices. But not father, nor Foley nor Ransome!

The rock fragment had been moved, stolen from father and taken somewhere else! These were enemies, guarding the rock upon the top of which we stood fatuously waving our little black and white flags!

CHAPTER 27

THE FIGHT ON THE ROCK SUMMIT

Alt who was standing with Dianne and Ahlma, must have realized from my attitude that something was wrong. I stood stammering, clutching at Drake. Then I got it out.

"Hide, Drake! This isn't our room—that's not father up there!"

We swung back, and I shouted, "Alt, back!"

Alt had already drawn the girls into the shelter of an overhanging rock. We crouched for a moment, not daring to move. Had we been seen from above? A blast of poisoned liquid from a spray up there could kill us here instantly. Or a monstrous finger could come down with a swoop and mash us.

Drake murmured, "Shall we take the diminishing drug? Make a run for it, and back?"

Failure. It beat at me. All our plans gone down into defeat. This was defeat—death for us. A retreat into the abyss; but we would meet the Togarites coming out! And where was father? What had happened up here?

Alt whispered, "We must get back in."

Drake gripped me. "Are you sure, Frank? Father may have changed things around. If we go back in, without knowing—that's the end, Frank! The end for us all; for the Mitans, depending on us. What will we do?"

The girls crouched, silent, white-faced. It was only a moment or so. We never reached a decision—it was forced upon us. From the edge of the rocky slope near at hand a man's head and shoulders appeared! A man about our own size! He was climbing up from the plain upon which the rock lay. A long bar of metal, thin as a sword, was in his teeth.

He was a hatless, bullet-headed Togarite, a heavy-set fellow, naked to the waist, with dark hair matting his thick chest. He saw us! He shouted and others appeared behind him. Four of them altogether.

Of us all, Alt was the one who had most presence of mind. The Togarite shouted at us. Alt understood the words. He shoved the girls lower behind the rock; he snatched my flag, and stood up, waving it. I caught his words to Drake.

"They don't know if we're friends or enemies."

The rock was, as I had feared, out of father's possession. But it was being guarded now by a method wholly different. The giants in the room overhead had doubtless not yet seen us. They were, I guessed, not overly alert, because four of their men in this smaller size were down here watching for any who might come.

Instant, swift impressions. I realized that Togaro was expected. The Togarites were coming. It would be difficult to tell a friend from an enemy—and so the guards were put into this smaller size.

Alt waved our flag, and shouted something in his own language. The Togarites stood in a group, twenty feet away, regarding us; four of them, with drug belts, and armed with the swordlike bars. They seemed impressed with our flag. They called again to Alt, and again he answered. To us, Alt flung over his shoulder:

"Doubting us, Drake! If I get them over here, leap upon them. They are only four."

We were three. But Drake had an automatic. He said softly, "Yes, Alt! Closer—we must get them all. Then, if we're not seen from above—"

The Togarites were cautiously advancing. Then they must have seen Dianne! Recognized her golden robe perhaps. They stopped, and then with menacing shouts came running at us.

Alt flung down his flag. "Now!" He made a rush, with Drake and me after him. Drake's automatic spat. The leading Togarite stumbled, fell and lay motionless. The others leaped over him. Drake raised his weapon again; but one of the Togarites flung a bar. It struck Drake's arm. The automatic clattered away; Drake and the fellow locked together and went down, rolling on the ground.

The other two rushed at Alt. He met them full. I was close behind him. His fists flew; he caught one of his assailants in the face. But the other struck with the bar. It must have landed upon Alt's head. He crumpled.

I was gripped by the fourth Togarite—the one Alt had hit. His bar missed me. I caught at his arm; held it, tried to wrench away his weapon. We struggled on the uneven ground. He was a burly fellow. I wound my legs around him, and suddenly he stumbled and fell. I twisted and came down on top, but could not hold him. His lunge heaved me up. I was flung sidewise, but as I scrambled, my hand seized a metal bar which had been dropped. I clung to it.

Then the other Togarite leaped upon me. He was finished with Alt. He jumped upon me as I was trying to rise. I rolled, with the two of them pounding at me. The bars were thin but heavy things. I warded a blow from my head. Then my hand with the bar hit one of the men. He fell away from me.

I was aware of Drake shouting, "Coming, Frank!"

My remaining antagonist had me by the throat. He was half on top of me. Beyond his ugly distorted face I saw Drake rising—and the Togarite under him lay inert.

I was pinned. My breath was stopped. In another moment I would have been unconscious. But Drake came with a leap. He had seized his automatic where it lay on the rocks. The butt of it crashed against the skull of the man over me.

My senses faded, but came instantly back. Drake was pulling the body off me. He helped me up. Around us lay the four Togarites, motionless. Alt was lying here also. And Alt, I thought, was dead.

Dianne and Ahlma came running forward.

We stood a moment breathless, confused, undecided what to do. The white-faced, trembling girls bent over Alt. The blow on the head had perhaps only stunned him. But there was a sharpened bar of metal now, sticking gruesomely in his side.

The thing had happened so swiftly! Overhead in some strange, monstrous room, giants were sitting. As Drake and I stood here in the silence, victorious in this fight, but with our dead friend here, the rumble of the talking giants overhead was plainly audible. To them, all this was a tiny combat, fought upon a quarter of an inch of rock surface. They had not yet seen or heard us, not realizing that anything unusual was transpiring on the small chunk of rock at their feet. Ants may fight in deadly combat and the human, whose shoes is their battle ground may be all unaware of them.

I pulled myself together. "Drake, we've got to hide these bodies! Perhaps we can avoid discovery."

There were many recesses here. We dragged and tumbled the bodies out of sight, or at least what we hoped would be out of sight of the people overhead.

Drake panted, "We'll have a few minutes, maybe. But they're likely to discover that their guards are gone."

"Drake, let's not go back in. We've got to get out, Drake! Out to the world with these drugs—and with a warning of what is coming."

"And get to father. Oh, Frank—"

He did not finish. Had father been killed?

"We'll get out," I said. "Here, put these vials in your belt, you've got more room." We were despoiling the dead Togarites of their drug supply. We hurried from the last one, back to where Alt lay with Dianne and Ahlma over him. They were in plain sight from above.

"Carry him somewhere, Drake. We mustn't be seen—above everything, not be seen. Is he dead, Dianne?"

She answered, with a surprising hushed calmness, "No, not yet. Our poor friend!"

We lifted him up, as quietly as we could. In a small ravine with a jutting rock above it, we laid him down.

"The best we can do, Drake."

CHAPTER 28

THE RETURN TO EARTH

"Not that way, Frank! Let's get around the back—I think it's a better chance."

We had clambered down the ten feet of jagged rock. We didn't change size—we had to risk it as we were, for to have got smaller would have made the descent too great. Somehow we were not discovered. We seemed to be on the floor of a room. A stone floor—we saw it as a ridged, uneven rocky plain. Off in the distance was what might have been a table, chairs, and the legs of seated men.

Ahead of us, a quarter of a mile away, was a cliff-like precipice. I figured it to be the wall of the room. It seemed darker over there.

We ran. The rock had a small fence around it—a fence which, compared to the normal room-size, was probably a foot or two high. We darted through its bars. In five minutes, perhaps, we were in the shelter of the bottom of the wall. It was seemingly of rocks and earth, piled and plastered together. It was dank with moisture, but solid to us in this size.

We stood a moment in the shadows here, panting from the run.

"Where do you suppose this is?" Drake demanded. "Can you make any-thing out of it, Frank?"

We were secure for the moment. It was dark over here. Standing with quiet survey I could imagine that there were three or four men off there in the distance. That this was a room with a single light overhead. No window on this side. The other walls were too far away to be visible.

"The door," said Drake. "That's what we've got to find—got to get out through it."

But where were we? Certainly this was no room in our home. It looked as though it might be a place hastily, amateurishly built. But it was tight. No crevices—no cracks or openings. The bottom of this wall was plastered solid with wet mud. The air down here was dank and heavy with moisture.

Dianne murmured, "Listen! That sounds like water."

A strange, muffled reverberating roar sounded from some great distance. A giant sea pounding? It seemed like that. My heart sank. Why this could be a place very far from King's Cove. The wild thought came to me—was this an earthly sound, this muffled pounding of the sea.

I said something like that to Drake.

"Nonsense! They've stolen the rock, Frank, and built this hiding place— probably not far from King's Cove. Where could they go?"

Dianne said abruptly, "I think this is all very small—this place they've built down here."

It was a new idea to us. But it seemed probably true. The Togarites would be in hiding. They had stolen the rock, made it small, and built this tiny housing place.

Our escape was still undiscovered. Not far from us was a long, slanting shadow—as though a table perhaps were cutting off the light. We walked until the shadow was upon us. And by the wall along here was a neglected pile of caked mud, large as a house to us. We found an opening like a cave-mouth, and squeezed in.

We were momentarily safe. "You stay here with the girls," I suggested to Drake. "I'll get large enough to see what the place looks like and how we can get out."

A discussion in the room interrupted us. The rock was visible a quarter of a mile away. A figure was growing upon it, expanding swiftly. A man. He leaped from the rock. We could see him moving in the opposite direction from us, reaching the little fence, climbing over it.

He had shouted. The distant giant shapes had sprung into action. They seemed bending down. There was surprise, but no turmoil.

"Togaro!" murmured Ahlma.

It was Togaro. As he expanded, there was a size when, with the light upon him, we saw him plainly. There had been no guards to challenge him. He had come swiftly out of the rock and was large enough when he first shouted to enable the men in the room to recognize him. He was standing off there now, growing to their size. We could hear the rumble of their voices.

It changed our plans. The fact that the guards were missing would now be discovered.

"We can't stay here," said Drake. "If they suspect us, they'll begin searching."

Nor could we run the miles along the walls of this room, hoping to find an open door. We decided we would have to dare a slightly larger size. We stood in the comparative darkness beside this cake of mud and grew—

The room, in a moment, had dwindled. We huddled against its wall. We knew that at any moment we might be discovered, but we had to take the risk. It was a small, windowless cell to its other occupants, though still gigantic to us.

Four men, and Togaro, stood by a table of stone. There was a closed door in the opposite wall. Two men stood by it. A light now sprang over it, so that the room over there was brightly illuminated.

Ahlma heard them, "Togaro is saying his first party is coming out now."

They were already coming! The rock seemed much closer to us now, and smaller. Tiny figures showed on its summit. They leaped down, they stood expanding.

It was at once a dismaying and welcome diversion. The missing guards were forgotten in the turmoil of the arriving Togarites. A hundred or more of them came. The room was in confusion. They tramped about while we shrank again into our niche. They grew large, and in parties of ten, were checked through the door, passing under the light to the darkness outside.

The turmoil made it easier for us. We got around the wall, near to the door. It was a long march, for near the end when we were sure of our direction, we shrank again to a smaller size, and kept close against the wall so that we might not be trampled.

The Togarites were pouring now from the rock. This was the arrival of the first thousand. They seemed so formidable as they grew gigantic and jammed the room! Giant hordes, arriving here on earth! The conquest had begun!

It made us realize anew that with the world harried by these giants, possession of the drug was of vital importance. The drugs were Togaro's chief weapons. But we four had them also. If we could get out of here—get quickly to the authorities and deliver the drugs—it might be the difference between defeat and victory for the world.

We may have stood there an hour. The arriving Togarites poured into the room; they marched through the doorway in a steady stream.

But we did not dare try to slip through. The light was bright, and there were two guards with gaze always upon the floor. From where we lurked we could see outside; a dim vista of blurred, luminous darkness and crowding giant figures. There was a babble of rumbling voices, both outside and in here.

An hour passed.

Then came the chance we had felt must come at last. The bodies of the Togarites we had killed on the rock summit were discovered! A group of the arriving people carried them down. Togaro had been moving about the room. His voice rang out with commands.

Ahlma translated: "He says, 'Close the door!' No more people are to come now from the rock! Oh, Drake, they're going to search for us! They know now that we are here!"

The guards sprang to the sliding door. But that act momentarily took their gaze from the floor. We were, to them, a few inches high. We were desperate. The door slid closed; but we had made a wild dash and gone through!

We found ourselves outside, in what seemed an outdoor darkness. A void, with a sheen of distant silver light far overhead. Giants trampling about. We dashed for a great jagged porous column. It was wood. We hid in one of its cave cells—a broken niche in its side. There was no search going on out here for us. The giants were tramping about, moving away.

Presently we dared to increase our size again, when the space out here seemed cleared momentarily of the tramping figures. Of all the size-change we ever experienced, I think that this was now the most surprising. The giants in the distance seemed also growing. We could hear them, but soon realized that another wall was between us and them. We were, for the moment, alone.

We had taken only a taste of the enlarging drug.

"Where are we?" exclaimed Drake. "How small are we?"

The pounding of the distant sea had been louder out here. But now, as we grew, it shrank until presently it was a murmur. Not a roar, far away—but a murmur, near at hand. The gentle lapping of water, close somewhere here.

And we found a tiny, mound-like house of sand and mud shrinking at our feet. It was sheltered by an overhanging arch of rock. The room from which we had escaped! It dwindled and was gone into smallness.

A rush of madness swept me as I saw that tiny mound. A kick of the toe of my shoe would crush it. Kill Togaro and all his men in there. But the madness passed. For all I knew, father might be in there. And the rock certainly was down in there. If I stamped, that tiny grain of rock would be forever lost. And a hundred thousand Mitan refugees were in it, waiting for Drake to return to them with help!

Other walls closed in around us. The giants were obviously outside of them. A floor became apparent—a floor of earth and sand, and near by there was a vast spread of uneven wood. As we grew, it shrank to planking. A void of darkness was beyond it. No, not darkness! A patch of silver sheen. Water, off there. Water, with moonlight on it; water, lapping gently under this planking on which we were now standing.

Dawning recognition was coming to us. The rough boards; walls; this ceiling close over us, with timbered beams; this archway, with shining water beyond it—it was the interior of our own boathouse on the shore of King's Cove!

It was night—a calm, placid night of moonlight on the water. The boathouse was empty, save for ourselves as at last, in a normal size to earth, we stood in a corner.

Our dory was gone. The slip of water here was vacant. Outside the boathouse we heard the throng of Togarites tramping about the cove!

CHAPTER 29

THE THEFT OF THE ROCK

It was the night of May 14 when Alt had come from the rock with his white flag of truce, and had taken me back into the atom with him. Togaro had been lurking outside; he had got into our guarded room. He had ridden me into smallness. Alt and I had not been aware of him. Father and Foley, watching us dwindle upon our journey, had not seen him.

But he was there; and he had leaped off me—small as an insect—and escaped. I have recounted the incident. It was in the caldron valley, not far below the upper surface of the rock fragment. I have described how we met a Togaro giant, who apparently was on his way out.

It seems obvious to me now that Togaro, when he was hidden upon me during that hour or so while Alt and I made the first stage of our inward journey, had been able to overhear our conversation. I recall that I told Alt then how I had arranged with father that, coming back, we would use a black and white flag as a signal. As a matter of fact, Togaro also was probably within our guarded room when father, Foley and I had discussed it.

He knew, then, about the flag. He escaped from Alt and me, in the caldron. He had seen and recognized his follower—had been clinging to me when we encountered and fought the giant. That fellow was on his way out, looking for Togaro, very probably, to see why the master was delayed all those months. There must have been near by other Togarites with him upon the journey, and Togaro escaped from us in order to join them.

I do not know any of this to be a fact; I construct it only in the light of what actually transpired afterward; and I think that doubtless it is what happened. Togaro met his men, told them the rock was in hostile hands, and told them of our flag signal. Then he ordered them out to capture the rock from father.

I can even fancy that Togaro lingered to aid in that capture, for it was very swiftly done; then, finding it successful, he had hastened back into smallness. Alt and I were inept at the size-change traveling. We made many blundering miscalculations; it would not have been difficult for the skillful Togaro to overtake us and to hide upon our ship as he did.

Thus Togaro, with the knowledge that the rock was in his possession, was enabled to bring his expedition up with utter confidence. Dianne and I had marveled at his assurance.

I think this is the true explanation. In any case, the fact remains that the rock was swiftly captured from father. Alt and I departed at about midnight of May 14. Father watched us go. He was depressed, harassed, over my going. He watched until Alt and I were no longer visible. Then he went to bed, leaving Foley on guard.

What happened to Foley, no one will ever know. Father lay in his room, with the alarm bell beside him. He could not go to sleep for a long time. Then he must have dozed.

He was awakened by the violent ringing of the bell. Foley calling him that there was danger! It was near dawn; father noticed the daylight through his bedroom windows. He had not undressed; he seized his automatic and rushed down the hall.

He was too precipitate, confused by being awakened too suddenly. The bell was clanging through the silent house with the urgency of a fire-alarm. Father burst incautiously into the room where Foley had been guarding the rock. He remembers seeing the body of Foley upon the floor. Three or four strange men were in the room—one large, the others very much smaller. The one of father's stature had a crudely fashioned black and white flag in his hand—with which, undoubtedly, he had deceived Foley.

Father fired point-blank as he blundered into the room. He evidently missed. The man with the flag flung it. The flagstaff was a bar of metal; it struck father's head and knocked him senseless.

Ransome was due to arrive to relieve Foley at seven in the morning. He came and found Foley dead, with a sharpened bar like a sword impaled in him. Father was lying there unconscious.

The room was in no disorder. Father's automatic was beside him. The granite slab was in its place.

But the fragment of rock was gone!

This was during the week of May 15. The local authorities were skeptical of father's story. Even with the public facts of the previous year—the coming of the giants, the battle on Bird's Nest Island—what father now said was incredible. This atom, within the rock, as the source of the inexplicable "giants," was to these local officials too much for belief. Heaven knows, one cannot blame them—especially since the rock had vanished and no one remained who had ever seen it, or even heard of it, save father and Ransome.

Father was taken to Portland for treatment. When he had recovered, the authorities at Washington sent for him. Officialdom there placed more credence in what he had to say; but not enough to do anything about it! As a matter of fact, what could they have done?

On the night of May 20, with father still ill, and in Washington with Ransome to give their testimony, our place at King's Cove was unoccupied. The Togarites poured from the tiny rock, a thousand of them in this first party. They grew into the boathouse, then left it, and roamed over King's Cove in the moonlight, still growing.

It must have been near dawn, when the first of them came out. Togaro was presently with them, I have no doubt. What they did was far different from the sporadic appearance of those giants of the year before. Organized, intelligent action now!

Shortly after that dawn of May 21, the world rang with the news that giants had come again. In Washington, the officials with whom father had been in consultation knew now that everything he said was the truth.

The menace was at hand! The world was fronted by the strangest, gravest crisis of its civilized history!

CHAPTER 30

THE WORLD AT BAY

I can give only a broad picture of those events which followed during May. They are history today. I saw them, as presently I will explain, from an inside viewpoint; a narrow viewpoint indeed. But as the world saw them, so were they now unfolded to father.

The dawn of May 21 showed giants rising from King's Cove. The first reports were contradictory and confused. But the giants were there! They were apparently about two hundred feet tall. A score of them at first. Then more—a hundred or so.

The few people who lived in the vicinity of King's Cove took instant flight. There were at first no casualties except a woman who fainted and an aged man who died of heart failure running with his family along the road toward Elton.

The giants did nothing menacing. They seemed busy moving about the neighborhood. They trampled it. Cleared it. Spreading out over a mile or so of territory along the water front. A plane passed overhead and reported that they appeared to be occupying the territory, not in haphazard fashion, but with a rational, methodical planning.

By noon the reports were coming in with more coherency. There had been a few ships in the channel. They had seen the giants, and had hastily steamed away. The passing planes brought the most detailed news. By noon, no airplane passed King's Cove at its accustomed level. They all were bending aside and flying high. But one or two of the passengerless mail planes flew low enough for close observation, and within a few hours both the American and Canadian governments were sending out official flyers to observe and report.

There was chaos that morning. No official orders were given to attack the giants—indeed there was no force available which dared attack them. By noon, it was father's opinion that any organized attack, until more was known of the conditions, would be a mistake.

The Togarites quite evidently were proceeding with definite purpose. By noon, a line of two-hundred-foot giants were stationed at intervals along the shore front. They stood, or sat calmly upon the cliffs. They were half a mile apart—ten of them over a five-mile length.

Then their line turned inward. At half mile intervals they took up their posts. A curving line, embracing the town of Elton and several others. There had been an encounter at Elton. All the towns were within a few hours abandoned. The whole of this five-mile area—and ten or fifteen miles shoreward—was abandoned. But at Elton some stray group of people had been trapped. A giant ahead of his fellows, had come wandering up. He was shot at by rifles and shot-guns. And hit, evidently, for he raised his leg, and he let out a cry of pain. He kicked at a house and demolished it. But he made no effort to fight. He stood nursing his leg where the bullets had stung it, and watched the people as they fled away.

There was a giant stationed up every road where it entered the Togarite territory. For a few hours, automobiles with panic-stricken refugees occasionally dashed out. The giants let them pass unmolested.

Such were the reports that first morning. The observation planes told that the captured area was bustling with activity. The giants seemed unarmed, and without belts of drugs. There were not many of them. But around King's Cove were throngs of Togarites in a smaller size—a size, it was said, about normal to earth. They occupied our house and all the other houses of the neighborhood. By evening they had marched to the deserted towns.

A rational occupation of this captured territory. And it was said that they seemed moving, and installing equipment, erecting their own dwellings. What seemed brown, conical tents were appearing. Firewood was being gathered. An encampment of war; with families of men, women and children—noncombatants making themselves comfortable for a permanent stay.

A thousand people. But soon it was obvious that they were far more numerous than that. All day they were appearing—growing from a tiny size. Hordes of them. By nightfall it was said that there were several thousand. Presently it was identified that the source of them was the Ferrule boathouse on the shore of King's Cove.

The night of May 21-22 would have been moonlit, but the moon and stars were obscured by clouds. But the Togarites' territory was not dark. Floodlights of some unknown current brightened it with spots of yellow from wire grids which the giants set up at intervals. The lighting systems of the captured towns were out of commission, but the Togarites quite evidently had their own power.

A weird scene of activity by night. There were camp fires everywhere. The area was thronged with the arriving enemy. Unearthly, fantastic scene! It was an encampment of little people, patrolled by watchful giants.

By the morning of the twenty-second, the Togarite lines had spread. A single giant—five hundred feet tall perhaps—made a rush southward. As though to clear the territory, he ran toward Portland—came to its outskirts, stopped and strode back. There had been an exodus from Portland the day before, and few were left in the city. The giant did not enter. He went back the way he had come—along the coast—leaving a trail of devastated towns in his wake.

I think that this giant may have been Togaro himself, for the reports said that he wore a belt of drugs—and several times was observed to change his size. His foray was doubtless to make sure that the territory southward was clear of inhabitants. Then his lines came down. The giants marched calmly along the coast—with a similar line of them some ten miles inland.

The city of Portland was occupied by the Togarites on the 23rd of May. It was an orderly advance, made during the night.

The next day, the lines again moved southward.

I find it difficult in these limited pages, to portray a broad enough picture. A myriad abnormal events were taking place throughout the world. I can only sketch them at random. The organized dissemination of news, for which our age is famous, proved now a grave menace to public safety. The giants, in those first few days, probably actually killed not more than a few hundred people. But the broad-casted news that giants were upon earth—human enemies capable of growing to limitless size—that fact publicly known was responsible for the death of many thousands.

There were panics—street crowds trampling their fellows—thousands of miles from any giants. A disorganization of all normal activity. But it was worst, of course, in eastern Canada, and the Atlantic seaboard of the United States. In New England it was chaos. A flight, with cities abandoned, roads thronged with refugees, transportation overloaded.

Trains, vessels, and the air lines struggled to cope with broken schedules and a mad rush of frenzied passengers. Accidents of every sort were reported—but in the mass of extraordinary happenings with which the news-tape was jammed, they passed almost unnoticed.

Within a few days, when it became evident that the enemy was moving southward, Boston was depopulated, as was all of Cape Cod, and every city and village along the coast.

Father stayed in Washington. He had immediately advised against a premature attack of Togaro. Even had Washington overruled him, no attack could have been made in those first days, for every official thought and effort was absorbed by the need of transportation. Millions of people were routed from the threatened territory. This was unlike any war the world had ever known. Advancing enemy armies had always found the great bulk of the civilians remaining in captured territory.

But there was no living soul willing to remain within a hundred miles of these giants. A psychological terror—and the very real danger of being trampled upon.

Transportation was of vital importance. Government airplanes, ships, soldiers and police were all absorbed in helping the people to escape. There was little thought of attacking this enemy.

Yet there had been sporadic encounters. A battleship had put into Boston harbor, with the intention of helping transport the people. A giant, ahead of his fellows, had come wading down the coast. There were still some people in the city of Lynn. He stamped upon them, and wrecked the snug little city, green and beautiful in the spring sunlight. Within five minutes it was a burning mass of wreckage. Then the lone giant came on southward.

The battleship, whose commander perhaps felt that he was trapped, turned and steamed out of Boston harbor. Then it faced the giant, and shelled him from a distance of a few miles.

The giant, whose head and shoulders were some fifty feet above the ocean as he waded near shore, was struck and killed. His body stained the water, lashed it to bloody foam with his dying struggles.

But from the north another giant rose. Again I think it must have been Togaro. He grew to a size monstrous and came leaping down the coast. Some reports have it that he was a thousand feet tall; others say still higher. He bounded from one village to another in a single leap. Then he dived into the ocean and swam.

The battleship was trapped by the hook of Cape Cod. It fired a single broadside—and missed, for the swimming Togaro saw the smoke-puff of the guns, and dived in a watery cataclysm.

He came up close to the ship. He flung an arm over it. Like a toy, the great battleship up-ended, was heaved up into the air, and sank.

There were a few survivors, for Togaro ignored them as though they were ants struggling in a pond. He turned, swam north—waded ashore and dwindled into the northern distance.

No more attacks were made on the Togarites by sea. This act of reprisal—so obvious, and so successful—gave the government pause.

But there was, that same day, an attack by a group of Canadian planes. Whether it was officially planned or not I cannot say. A group of planes, six or eight of them, came down from the border and flew over the enemy territory.

This was now about five o'clock in the afternoon. The giants stared up at the invading planes, but did not seem to heed them. The planes were emboldened. Perhaps the pilots figured that these giants could not grow upward fast enough to overtake them. A plane could rise in a few moments to a height of fifteen or twenty thousand feet. No giant could do that.

The little squadron of lead-colored war planes flew into the heart of the Togarite territory. The center of it, at this time, was inland from Portland. The planes came low—and one of them dropped a bomb from a height of under a thousand feet. It struck one of the standing giants. Wounded but probably did not kill him.

The planes zoomed up and away. They dropped other bombs. One fell into the city of Portland.

But none of the planes escaped. These supposedly unarmed giants were most efficaciously armed—with the sling-shot! I have already had occasion to mention it. In the hands of a two-hundred-foot giant, it was a sling thirty or forty feet long. It flung, not a pebble, but a rock huge as a bowlder, with a speed almost of a bullet.

Giants leaped into action beneath the soaring planes. To them, the planes were toys, flying only a few times higher than the length of their own bodies. With skilled marksmanship they flung their rocks. The planes were struck. One by one they came crashing down.

CHAPTER 31

TOGARO STRIKES

Father sat that night in the War Department at Washington. He had been in constant consultation with the authorities, for he, more than anyone in the world, could explain what manner of people were these Togarites. Yet even father knew very little.

"We can't stand up against warfare like this!" exclaimed the war secretary.

There were orders given that night that under no circumstances were the Togarites to be attacked. Reprisal by the enemy was too easy—too efficacious.

Additional warnings to the public were issued. The enemy was moving slowly southward—the territory in advance of them was ordered abandoned. No need to enforce such orders! A wave of refugees rolled back, a hundred miles in advance of the slow-moving giant lines.

Indescribable scenes of confusion and terror marked those days toward the close of May. The Togarites moved largely at night; every dawn found them farther south. They crossed Massachusetts, and Rhode Island. The 1st of June found their outposts well into Connecticut, following the north shore of Long Island Sound. New Haven was trampled by a single giant, on June 1—the city wrecked in an hour.

There were changes now in the enemy tactics. In Maine they had been careful not to demolish the cities unduly. Their own people were settling there. But now, farther south, only the active warring giants advanced. They laid everything waste beneath their monstrous tread. An area a hundred miles wide had been wholly abandoned days before. The advancing giants waded into it; stamping, kicking—firing it by night with great torches. A blackened, wrecked swath of country stretched down from Maine.

The giants were larger now. As their territory expanded they took a larger size. It was systematically done. Each seemed to have his post—a few miles over which he paced back and forth—with one of his fellows coming south at intervals to relieve him. And the reliefs were always larger—with more miles of country to pace. By June 1 it was estimated that they stood some five hundred feet tall.

On June 1 they had reached Long Island Sound barely a hundred miles from New York City, where millions of people, in all the chaos, were still unable to get away. Giants had already crossed the Hudson. One of them stood in the river and lunged against Bear Mountain Bridge until he tore it loose.

For all that the United States and Canada did not dare attack, there were frantic preparations for war. The battle planes were made ready. The Canadians were massed on the border—and a great fleet of American planes assembled in New Jersey. Artillery units were mobilized. Infantry would be useless. It was used now to aid the flight of the civilian population. The evacuated areas in advance of the giants were always under martial law, patrolled by soldiers who retreated slowly before the oncoming enemy.

The forts of the Highlands near the Hook—entrance to the port of New York—were ready to do what they could; and the forts at Wadsworth, on Staten Island, were ready.

The Atlantic battle-fleet was massed in the Chesapeake. The Pacific fleet was hastening through the Panama Canal.

Resistance seemed so useless! By virtue of size alone, this enemy was irresistible. Monstrous, terrible weapon of size! No one, contemplating it, could even have approximated the terror of the reality.

Yet it seemed horrible to do nothing. Father describes innumerable conferences in Washington, where the harassed government strove to plan what might be done. Nor was our government alone. The world was at stake. Every foreign government was frightened, offering help and advice.

Help was coming. Transport planes, bringing volunteers from Britain, were daily arriving. They flew the far-south route—landed in the Carolinas, and were rushed North.

A united, civilized earth opposed this enemy of giants. But to realize the desperate futility of it, one had only to envisage it from the giant viewpoint. A little, miniature world, like an anthill, outraged. Why, a single giant—Togaro alone—if he made himself large enough, could destroy this anthill activity!

Father recalls how our war secretary gripped him. "But what does he want, Ferrule? This Togaro—conquer us? God, man, we can't yield up our whole country! Our whole earth! Does he want to exterminate us? Why doesn't he say something, communicate with us, make demands—an ultimatum—terms for surrender—something! Anything, but not this gruesome silence!"

Father was silent. But to him came the wistful thought of Drake, Dianne and me. He wondered where we were—if only we would come back to him! If we had the drugs, and brought them now, the earth might be saved.

Warfare, with both sides using the drugs, would be terrible indeed. It might, probably would, destroy the world of its own momentum. Then there came to father with a flash of divination, the true aspect of what might happen if our earth forces had the drug. Togaro's giants never wore the drug-belts. Father could guess why. It was a weapon too powerful, so that Togaro did not dare entrust it now even to his own men. One, for instance, might be wounded, and in a frenzy take too much of the drug and run amuck, destroying all his fellows.

But there was another reason. A giant had already been killed. His body was floating in the ocean off Boston. Other giants might be killed. The Earth forces might get possession of the drugs.

Father wondered where the main drug supply was kept. Probably, he concluded, it was all upon Togaro's person. One man, controlling everything.

Father divined what might happen if the earth forces had the drugs. A general attack by our planes, our armies and navies, could be made. It might take the giants by surprise. A thousand of them—there seemed only that many—might be overcome. If Togaro could be separated from them so that they could be kept from growing larger, the earth-giants might fight with Togaro the combat of size.

Wild and desperate thoughts these. But father had them; and he prayed wistfully that Drake and I might come and bring with us the drug that would offer this last desperate hope.

This was the night of June 1 and 2. The dawn of the 2nd brought a new menace. In the ocean, far off at the curving eastern horizon beyond Sandy Hook, the head and shoulders of a giant loomed into the sky. No, not a giant, this—a titan. A monstrous, titanic thing in human form. Togaro! No one had seem him arrive. He swam down from Cape Cod, doubtless, in the darkness just before dawn, expanding as he swam.

And now he stood some twenty miles offshore. A mountain in the shape of a man off there. To observers at the sea-level he was standing beneath the curve of the horizon. And his torso loomed mountainous into the sky. A thousand feet? A mile? There are no eye-witnesses who can agree.

He stood a moment, and then he waded toward the Hook, and spoke. It was a rumble like distant thunder. It was heard all up and down the coast. Words blurred—but he said them over slowly. And they were heard, and then distinguished.

"I will talk now. I will tell you what to do."

The news was flashed to Washington. In the fort at Sandy Hook the commander of some gun-crew lost his wits and fired a shot. It struck Togaro in the shoulder. He stood with surprise and anger. Then he stooped and reached fumblingly into the ocean. He plucked up a dripping mass of rock and heaved it—a rock huge as the fort. It fell upon the Hook; the fortifications were buried beneath it.

There is no one who can tell with any coherency what happened in those next minutes. No one in New York could have seen more than the feet and towering legs of the infuriated titan as he bounded with splashing steps up the harbor. He wrecked the forts on Staten Island. He splashed into the upper bay and leaned over lower Manhattan. The Woolworth Building—a little toy reaching to his knees. The higher domes newly built along the Battery—they may have towered to the height of his thighs. He kicked at them. The falling masonry and steel fell into a litter at his shoe-tops—crashed and fell with what to him was a tiny clatter and a cloud of dust and smoke surging to his waist. He waded into it, for only a minute. Inconceivable wreckage!

He turned and strode back. A few of his leaps carried him down the harbor, churning up the Narrows, splashing through the Lower Bay, wading again into the ocean. The dawn was still behind him as he stood there. And again his roaring voice sounded:

"That will teach you not to attack me. Now I will tell you what to do!"

The incredible, inconceivable power of size!

An hour passed. Father was routed from his bed. In the War Department he found a throng of officials. The representatives of a dozen foreign governments were there. A turmoil with no attempt at any rational conference. The building rang with shouts:

"We must yield! This is madness. Hopeless."

A single enemy, armed only with the weapon of size, yet it was hopeless for all the world to try to fight him!

Togaro was still standing under the morning sky. His words were heard in New York, and flashed by wire to Washington.

"I command that you leave the United States. Take your people out of it as quickly as possible. I will not interfere with your retreat. I command you to sail the warships of your world—anchor them off the coast of Maine so that I may sink them."

He gave a score of details. He spoke for what was perhaps ten minutes. He ended:

"If you yield, send a plane now as a signal. Let it come near me—so that I may catch it in my hand. I will not kill its pilot."

There was a sudden heavy silence in that War Department room when the message came. Then someone said:

"Shall we yield?"

It meant giving over the whole world to this tyrant. Every man in the room knew it. And would it help? The wreckage at Lower Manhattan—those ten minutes just now at dawn—would yielding up the world spare other scenes like that? Or would this monster be insatiable?

"Shall we yield?"

The white-faced men whispered it to each other. The fate of their whole world, now in this breathless moment to hang upon their hasty, frightened decision.

They were spared the necessity of answering. A secretary burst in from the adjacent corridor.

"Ferrule! Dr. Ferrule!"

A message for father! A telephone from Mount Vernon in the northern suburbs of New York City, close now to the enemy lines.

Drake Ferrule had been found! He and a strange girl named Ahlma! They were safe. A plane had been sent to them, and they were coming to Washington.

And the message for father, from Drake:

"Don't yield! We're coming with the drugs."

Under the strain of it, the war secretary broke. He burst into an hysterical laugh. "Don't yield! Why, of course we won't yield! Attack them now— we're ready!"

The orders went out. Father tried to stop it. "Wait! Get the drugs first!"

But in the pandemonium around him he was unheeded. The attack had long been planned. The war planes were ready, massed in all the Jersey airports. The artillery units were ready. The roads and the railways of New Jersey were open and ready for swift transportation.

An attack upon the Togarite lines where they crossed, west of the Hudson, at the New Jersey border!

And off in the ocean beyond Sandy Hook, the titanic figure of Togaro stood waiting for his answer. But now, behind him, farther out and to the north, other huge figures were swimming! He did not at first see them. Two figures—expanding as they swam, coming to attack him! Then one of them stood on the ocean bottom; stood upright, towering into the sky. A figure almost as huge as Togaro.

The figure of a girl! A girl in a golden robe!

CHAPTER 32

THE FUGITIVES

It was near the dawn of May 21 when Drake and I, with Dianne and Ahlma, crouched in our boathouse at King's Cove. Giants seemed everywhere outside, towering figures in the moonlight, tramping about the cove.

I think that our best chance to escape from the Togarite territory was offered us there at the beginning—those first minutes just before dawn. We had the drugs. We might have plunged into the channel, swimming out, expanding our size and taking the chance that we would not be discovered too soon.

How easy to look back on what one might have done! But instead of that we crept from the boathouse and turned inland. Ran back from the cove. Past our house; Togarites in our normal size were thronging it.

We were confused. Behind us, giants were rising everywhere. People were pouring from the boathouse.

"If we can get to Elton—" Drake panted. We found the road and dashed along it. The moon was momentarily under a cloud. The concealing darkness was helpful.

A giant went past us. We ducked off the road. He did not see us—he strode toward Elton.

We started again. Then the moon came out. We did not dare use the open road. We skulked through the fields. Then the moon was paling with the coming dawn. We had not escaped. Giants were ahead of us, and to the sides.

We crouched by a fence and argued. If we got large, we might in a few moments dash out of this captured territory. But we would be seen at once—pounced upon.

If we got smaller, we would be safe from discovery.

But Drake was vehement against it. "Damn it, Frank, I've had enough of that! It'd be a journey of a hundred miles just to Elton, when we're smaller! I tell you we've got to get out of here quickly! Frank, these drugs are vital to the world."

It seemed that our best chance was in our normal size. The dawn came. We found a dilapidated barn on a side road halfway to Elton. We hid in it.

We were, with the daylight upon us, hopelessly caught within the Togarite lines. It was soon obvious that getting to Elton would not help us. Giants were already there. We thought, if we could head inland, but then south, toward Portland, we might get past them.

So many things we might have dared to do are apparent, looking back upon it now! We struggled—all those days in May—to get to civilization somewhere, to find transportation south to New York. We had the vital weapon—the one thing the world could successfully use against this enemy. Because it was so important, we were afraid to chance anything. If Togaro caught us, the world was doomed. Terrible responsibility! An excess of caution was upon us.

We skulked and hid by day, and traveled at night. But there were always giants around us. Patrolling watchfully in the daylight, and at night with their lights and torches. It seemed that we could never escape those widening lines. Within a day or two we realized that we should have headed north; but it was too late now to change.

We tried to get to the coast. It was too dangerous; there were more giants that way than anywhere else. We had a hundred narrow escapes from capture. It was a problem to find food and water as we went. But there were deserted houses into which we slid by night.

Once we found an abandoned automobile. We ran it southward, all one night, dashing forward, stopping with lights out and silent motor when a giant approached. Then on again—until at last we barely were able to fling ourselves from it and take the diminishing drug, when a giant came up, stooped and tossed the car into the air. We lay in the bushes by the roadside and dwindled in size until the danger was past.

We lost count of the days on this strange flight. And we lost our way—wandered, following what roads we dared, working southward by what devious routes I have no idea. It seemed a hopeless journey. The country was now a torn mass of wreckage. Littered, burning towns. Roads obstructed. No storm of nature could ever devastate a countryside like this!

After more than a week of wandering, it seemed that we were still as far inside the spreading Togarite lines as ever. We had stolen garments to disguise the girls. We had several times tried getting larger. One dark night, when it chanced that the lights of the giants were not too near us, we traveled in a fifty-foot size for hours. It gained us so much distance that we tried it again several times. We passed inland from Boston, crossing into the desolation of what had been Rhode Island, then into Connecticut.

There came a night which, though we did not know it, was the evening of the 1st of June. We lay in the wreckage of a farmhouse which had been demolished. The girls were too exhausted to travel farther, and we all needed a rest. It had been the most fearful day of our trip. That morning we had been driven out of our hiding place where we intended to spend the daylight hours. It was an abandoned house near the edge of a town. What town I do not know.

Marauding giants had come and burned the town. We had escaped into smallness. It was night when after desperate efforts, we again emerged to find ourselves barely a hundred feet away from where we had been before.

The night came. We could not travel farther. One of us had always to be awake on guard. The girls were bravely standing the hardships, but they were both in miserable plight. They lay now, huddled in this shattered farmhouse. The broken roof was like a tent over us. We had had a meal, of food picked up along the way. We decided not to travel until the next night. The girls wrapped themselves in the men's overcoats we had found for them. They were soon asleep, huddled amid the litter of plaster and lath strewn around us.

Drake and I sat whispering. Drake wore now a single automatic. The girls and I were unarmed. The automatic was a futile weapon—a thousand times Drake cursed its futility; never once had we found any rational use for it.

"Where do you suppose we are, Frank?"

We had but the vaguest idea. But it was not far from the coast—Long Island Sound lay a mile or so off there.

"Not far from New York," I said. "This might be near Norwalk."

We had often been able to locate ourselves by broken street signs in the wrecked towns. At night sometimes, when we were in the fifty-foot size, we would poke about to find a railroad station which would have its name upon it.

It seemed now that the outposts of the captured territory must be close ahead of us. A line of standing giants had been visible down there. They had not yet entered New York City, we felt sure.

"We'd better try and get to the coast," Drake said. "If it weren't for the girls—" He shot a glance toward where they were sleeping. "Frank, I wish we'd been able to find a plane, take a chance on getting out of here with one dash—"

"Well, we haven't found one," I retorted. There had been many, but they were all wrecked. "Besides, Drake, we decided that would be too dangerous. You remember those Canadian war planes."

We had seen that episode. We saw, indeed, so many strange things which I have no space here to mention!

I added: "If we had a plane we'd no more than get it into the air before we'd be struck. You know that."

He paused, then reached a sudden decision. "Frank, we'll rest here. But tomorrow night I'm going to make a break for it. You stay with the girls. They can't travel much farther."

He shot another glance at them. Was Dianne awake and listening to us now? I think so. I seem to recall that she stirred. But at the time we did not notice.

Drake went on vehemently. "We've got to do something—get the drugs to Washington. Why, Frank, in a few days New York City will be gone."

"What do you mean, make a break for it?"

"You stay with the girls. Keep hidden. No use to try to travel. Get yourself food and water and dig in somewhere and wait. And I'll get out—I can do it, Frank, alone."

"How?"

"Get large. We'll get over by the coast. I'll make a dash for it, swimming. They won't see me until I'm large enough to put up a fight. Frank, it should have been done long ago."

He was my older brother, I could not talk him out of it. And it did seem the only thing left for us to do.

"You go to sleep, Frank. I'll stand guard for awhile."

"You're not going to try it tonight?" I demanded, with anxious suspicion.

"No."

"You promise?"

"Yes, of course. I'm tired as hell. Go to sleep. We'll stay here all tomorrow."

Sleep came always to us the instant we relaxed. But this time, as though fate would have it so, I awakened within a few hours.

"Drake?"

"Yes."

He was sitting beside me; the girls were still asleep.

"Take your turn, Drake. I'm wide awake." He needed no urging. He rolled up near me without a word.

I sat motionless. We were half outdoors; the tilting fallen roof only partially covered us. I could see the stars.

I presently went outside. A starlit, moonless night, a few hours before dawn. No giants seemed in sight. A deserted, desolate, shattered countryside, wan and pitiful in the starlight. The thought flashed to me: might we not make a break for it now? No giants were near here at the moment.

But we had often tried that before, and there always was a giant within sight of us when we dared get larger.

I went back under the broken roof. Out of its other side, where the shattered wall had left a jagged opening, a small dark form was running.

Dianne! I caught a glimpse of her golden robe beneath the flap of the dark overcoat.

I stopped for nothing, but ran. Outside I called softly, "Dianne! Where are you going? Come back!"

There was a dim road. She was running along it.

I called again, but she did not stop, so I dashed after her.

I was overtaking her at first; then her strides lengthened and she drew away from me.

I gasped with horror, and fumbled at my belt. She had taken the drug; her running figure on the starlit road was growing larger!

CHAPTER 33

THE COMBAT OF TITANS

I need not concern these pages with further details of Drake and Ahlma. I have already made it clear that they escaped that same morning. Drake awakened, just before dawn, to find that Dianne and I were gone. He and Ahlma rushed outside. There was a commotion off by the coast. They stared at it, half understanding. Drake soon realized that his best move would be not to follow me.

He and Ahlma ran the other way, and took the fifty-foot size. They were desperate; and luck or Fate, as you will, was with them. The patrolling giants were standing in amazement, gazing off toward Long Island. Under ordinary circumstances of those past days Drake and Ahlma would have been attacked in a moment. But now the giants did not notice these fifty-foot figures running along the ground. The boundary of the Togarite lines chanced to be near here. A fifty-foot human runs with strides of thirty or forty feet. Drake and Ahlma, taking every chance now, clung to the open road.

They got past the Togarite area within half an hour. The giants all were behind them. The country was still devastated. Then the pair passed into an abandoned area, still intact, where the giants had not been, and crossed it.

They came at last, just after dawn, within sight of soldiers patrolling the edge of what still was civilization. Drake took the overcoat from Ahlma so that her robe would show. They dwindled to normal size; encountered the soldiers.

Civilization at last! A motor car took them to where a plane was available. Drake learned that father was in Washington—the whole world now knew father's name, and where he was, and what he had to say!

The telephone lines here were down. Drake found a way of sending a radiogram. But at that moment Togaro was devastating New York—in the chaos Drake's message was never delivered. The plane landed in Mount Vernon. Drake telephoned his message: "Don't yield—I have the drugs—"

Meanwhile, in the starlit darkness before dawn, I ran after the fugitive Dianne. She had taken the drug—I took mine also.

"Dianne!"

She saw that she could not shake me off. She stopped abruptly. She had cast away the overcoat because it impeded her running. I dashed up to her golden-robed figure. The trees were dwindling beside us; the open starlight was overhead.

"Dianne, are you crazy?"

"Go back, Frank!"

I was fumbling for the other drug. I pulled at her, but she resisted me.

"Frank, go back. Not two of us—Drake said one was best—he said it to you. He did say it. Frank, I mustn't stay here—I must run—run—"

But still I held her. She exclaimed:

"If you try to stop me, I'll call out!"

"Dianne, you promised me you'd be careful—not try a wild thing like this." I shook her. "Did you promise?"

"Yes. But I've changed my mind."

A madness was on her. She fought to escape me. "Let me go! Oh, Frank, I can make it! I can run very fast, and I know how to handle the drugs."

"No!"

"Then you come with me."

We were head and shoulders above the trees now. Across the dwindling fields I could see the open water of the Sound. A giant was to one side, a mile or so. He had seen us!

It was too late to retreat. Suddenly Dianne jerked away from me. I ran beside her, saying:

"We'll head for the water, straight over the fields."

"Yes, Frank."

A dozen giants who yet were larger than ourselves were near at hand, running at us.

Then they stopped and stared off toward Long Island. A monstrous figure rose up in the distant ocean; stood a moment, and then plunged again. Togaro, swimming down to New York!

Dianne recognized him. "Togaro!"

"Yes. Alone! Dianne, I think he's got all their drugs."

"We must get larger than he is!"

The water off Long Island Sound spread close ahead. Off to one side, down by our feet, a wrecked little village lay in the starlight. We were bounding along—Dianne ran like a fawn.

Giants—diverted momentarily by watching Togaro—were now closing in upon us. One fellow in advance of the others barred our way. I ran at him. His sling whizzed a pebble at me. It struck my shoulder. My fist caught his jaw. He toppled backward into the Sound. Dianne went past him, splashing.

I caught up with her. The other giants had retreated. They had no drugs, and we were now taller than they. Their slings flung a rain of pebbles after us.

We waded the Sound. The giants on Long Island kept away from us. We had grown well over five hundred feet now, and bounded across the little width of the island.

The dawn was coming. We stood gazing out over the placid ocean; it lapped with a foaming line of ripples on the narrow beach.

Togaro was down by Sandy Hook. His monstrous figure loomed up against the fading stars. He had not seen us, evidently. There was no way that these frightened giants near here could communicate with him.

We took more of the drug.

"If we can get as large as he is, Dianne—"

She pulled me down so that we crouched along the empty length of beach. A giant behind us flung a bowlder. But to us now it was small as a pea. It stung my face where it struck.

"Let's try swimming down," I murmured. "Take it slowly and wait until we get large enough to attack him."

My heart was thumping so that it seemed almost to smother me. This would be the supreme test. These Togarite giants to me now were dwindling pygmies. They had none of the drug. Helpless, futile little enemies. The Togarite hordes up in Maine? Why, they would soon be small as ants. The Earth forces, hovering on the outskirts of this little patch of devastated country, were only excited little gnats.

I laughed with a touch of hysteria as the power of my size surged over me.

"Dianne, all that back there amounts to nothing. We can control it. There's only Togaro!"

Just that single enemy left. We heard the rumble of his voice. We saw him stride toward New York City—his head and shoulders towering over the horizon level.

We swam beside a dwindling shore front.

"Dianne, you must keep close behind me."

Fear for her came upon me again. We were both unarmed, but so was Togaro, very probably. There was only the weapon of size.

"Don't go so fast, Dianne. Look, he's coming back from the city! Are we large as he is?"

She was swimming ahead of me.

"Try standing up, Dianne. See if you can wade yet. Dianne, wait! Keep behind me, I tell you!"

She was a faster swimmer than I. She did not heed me. The curve of the tiny island was beside us. A cove, with a headland a few feet high, was to our right—the entrance to New York harbor. A line of buoys, smaller than fishing bobs, lay on the water to mark the ship channel.

Togaro was farther out in the open sea. My foot touched the ocean bottom.

Dianne suddenly stood up. Then Togaro turned and saw us!

I called: "Dianne! Come back!"

Togaro was still somewhat taller than Dianne. He was what seemed a hundred feet from her. I was swimming frantically, twenty feet or so behind her. She and I were growing; and I saw Togaro's hand go to his mouth. He had taken more of the enlarging drug!

He stood for just an instant, surprised by our presence. Then he shouted: "You! Why—"

She made a rush forward, and dived into the water. With all my strength I swam. Togaro moved sidewise, then came at me. But Dianne suddenly appeared, rose up at his waist, where the water surged, and gripped him.

He bellowed: "Dianne—let go of me, you fool!"

She must have tripped him. He went down, splashing, roaring. I saw him strike her and heave her off.

I had stood up. The water was below my waist now. The little headlands of the land seemed only a few hundred feet away. I waded, and as Togaro shook Dianne loose and heaved himself upright, I closed with him.

He was a full head taller. His powerful arms went around me, bending me backward. His evil face leered at me.

"So, Frank Ferrule? You want to make a test like this? I'll kill you now—as I should have long ago."

He was horribly strong. His arms were crushing me. We were both expanding. We swayed and struggled, lashing the water white around us. His drug belt, with its water-tight metal vials, pressed against me. One of his legs went behind me, but I twisted, avoiding being thrown.

The water level was receding. It was down to our knees now. I straightened and got a hand under Togaro's chin. He suddenly cast me loose, and as I staggered and almost fell he leaped upon my back, forcing me down.

We had surged away from Dianne. I called frantically: "Dianne—keep off! You make it harder for me."

I found myself bent down by Togaro's weight, so that I was half sprawled upon a tiny shore front. A little line of cliffs the size of my hand. Fortifications here—a child's toy fort, smashed by a chunk of rock lying upon it.

I sprawled. There were humans here, frantic little insects running.

I managed to get up and twisted again to face Togaro. I got a blow in the face as we broke apart. But I gave one in return, then I hit him in the chest and ducked his swing.

Blood from my forehead where his knuckles had cut was in my eyes. I dashed it away.

I was more agile than Togaro with my fists; unskilled, yet I soon saw that I had more science than he. I gave him two blows for one, at the least. He staggered over and tripped on the cliffs of the shore.

But I knew it was a ruse. He had tried to clinch with me, but I was avoiding him. He knew I had him at a disadvantage if I could keep him away. He half fell, but instead of following I stepped backward. Dianne was beside me.

"Get back," she cried.

She had found a rock on the ocean bottom. She heaved it, dripping, at Togaro as he rose. It caught his shoulder, but did not seem to hurt him.

I gasped: "Dianne—back, for God's sake."

She obeyed me and retreated.

Togaro came at me again.

There was an instant as I stood there, waiting with raised fists to receive him, that a horrible sense of dizziness swept me. I felt myself standing a mile or two in the air. I could see down the lower bay, the Narrows—and see the wrecked buildings of Manhattan. All far below me, as though I were poised in a plane—this whole familiar scene dwarfed into miniature by my altitude.

Then my viewpoint changed. I was of normal size, standing here in a foot or two of water. This, at my feet, was a little green and brown model of New York harbor.

Togaro was rushing me. He hit me in the body. As I went a step backward from the impact he tried to grip me. But I was too quick; and as he rushed he launched a swing which, had it caught my chin, would have finished me. I ducked it. He slewed around with the effort. Then I hit him in the forehead. He stood swaying, then fell.

I was afraid to go near him. I stood away. He was up again in a moment. But there was a difference now. I was taller than he! My dose of the drug was still effective, but his had stopped!

He knew it was the end; defeat. I was ready with a blow that would have finished him, and he knew it. The expression on his face held me transfixed for an instant. A stupid, bewildered surprise. But that faded. There came something else. A look of regret as he flung a glance down at the tiny landscape? Regret, as he saw Dianne crouching behind me? If it were that, it was instantly gone. His hand went to his mouth!

A trick? But he leaped backward, flung up his arms with a gesture that stopped me again. He was staggering. He stood swaying, with one foot upon the few inches of the cliffs. The blood was draining from his face.

He had taken poison—his last titanic gesture!

He stood, and upon his livid, contorted face came a twisted leer of irony.

"Dianne, you win." From his belt he plucked a small globe of metal. "You win—but your—damned Mitans—lose!"

The fragment of rock was in that little globe! I knew it! As I leaped he flung the gleaming sphere over my head. It rose in an arc and fell into the sea. It must have burst with the impact. There was a puff. Within it, the tiny grain which held the Mitan world was lost forever.

Togaro kept to his feet a moment longer. He gasped again:

"You win—damn you both!"

Then he crumpled limply and fell at our feet, his monstrous body crashing down across the Highlands, and his head and shoulders sprawled far into the Lower Bay!

CHAPTER 34

PRINCESS OF THE COTTAGE

It seems that there is not much more I need record. A year has passed. It is summer again, and but for the fact I have lived those scenes over in my memory as I set them down here, they would seem remote indeed.

There was a mild turmoil, that morning of the second of June when the titanic body of Togaro came crashing down. Wild scenes of a tiny battle. But it was over almost before it started. Only the war planes, of all the earth forces, had time to get into action. They soared over the Togarite lines. But there was no courage left in the giants. They had no drugs. It was as we thought—Togaro kept upon his person the entire supply. The giants had seen his monstrous body fall—

They fought. Some of them were killed by the planes—and some of the planes were brought down. Then Drake entered the battle. He had seen from his rising plane at Mount Vernon what was transpiring. He hastily landed and took a heavy dose of the enlarging drug.

The giants fled before him.

The thing was over almost before Dianne and I could stride across the intervening tiny landscape to reach Drake. He had trampled some of the giants. But most of them he spared.

There was a day of wild confusion; but the Togarites were ready enough to do what they were told.

They were herded by Drake and me into Maine, then were reduced to normal earth size.

There is an island now where they, and the forty thousand followers with them, are isolated. Dianne and I have never been there. Dianne wants to forget the Mitans—those of her loyal people who were lost within the rock fragment.

The futile dragging of the Atlantic Ocean off Sandy Hook has proved unavailing. The rock must have been no larger than a grain of sand in that fragile globe which Togaro cast away. It is gone forever.

The drugs, too, are gone. The authorities very wisely decided it was too dangerous a thing to be allowed to exist on earth. The entire supply unanalyzed has been chemically destroyed.

It is June again now. One would hardly know that all these strange things happened only a year ago. The devastated area up through New England is looking better every week that passes. The countryside is green again in the summer warmth; the wrecked cities are repeopled and being rebuilt.

There was a gruesome task for Drake and me. In monstrous size we carried the dead body of Togaro as far out into the ocean as we could wade, then fastened rocks to it, and a rope. Then, swimming, we towed it a thousand miles farther and sank it into the ocean depths.

We want to forget all that now. When this narrative is finished—as it will be in a moment—I want to forget it forever. That was the past; the future holds so much of peace and beauty.

There is for me the glory of Dianne and her love.

We are living in a cottage by the sea. Drake and Ahlma live near us. Father is in New York. He says he would not live with a married couple—even with such beautiful and amiable daughters-in-law as Ahlma and Dianne. But he visits us often.

There is nothing of the princess about Dianne now, save that she is princess of our little cottage. We have no servant. When our family is larger we will have one, but just now Dianne is playing at housekeeping.

She was in here half an hour ago, urging me to stop my writing.

"It's nine o'clock, Frank. Bright moonlight. I'm going to build a fire. Camp fire—I've got clams. We'll bake them for Ahlma and Drake when they get back from the pictures."

"Right, Dianne. Go do that."

"But, Frank—"

"Get it started. Remember your signal fire on Bird's Nest? Let's make the signal again—like we used to when we were kids—"

"Come on."

"Can't—but I'll be through soon."

She went away, but she came back after awhile.

"The fire's built. Come on, Frank."

I imagine I ignored her. But she came again, just a minute ago.

She called in: "Oh, Frank!"

"Yes, Dianne?"

"Come on. Please stop."

"Presently."

"Frank Ferrule, you can make your own smoke signals for Drake and Ahlma. I'm going to bed."

I think I had better stop.